Praise for John Kinsella

"In Kinsella's poetry these are lands marked by isolation and mundane violence and by a terrible transcendent beauty." —Paul Kane, *World Literature Today*

"One of the greatest senses one gets reading across the breadth of Kinsella is not plenitude but particularity, a granularity revealed through the turning over of the same materials and revealing how subtle shifts in the way they lie against one another alters the sense of the whole. The introduction of any new element to the existent pool allows for thousands of new permutations." —*Westerly Magazine*

". . . a very talented & thoughtful poet . . ." —Charles Whalley

"Reading John Kinsella's [*Armour*] is something like reading a humanist, commonsense, political poet like Adrienne Rich–yet–in punk fashion–orchestrates musics like those of very different poets, such as J.H. Prynne, John Cage or Rae Armantrout." —*The Australian*

"Kinsella's handling of poetics of location, or home, brings to light an anarchical attempt to disown the ego heralded by the lyrical stance. His relinquishing of human centredness is ultimately impossible in human language and in human action, yet the intention and the objective give rise to an earth-centred poetics, which rewrites the human in place. Kinsella appears to negate any holistic apolitical realm by insisting on situated knowledge that positions a posthuman subject at play with non-human animals. This approach is not fashionable; it is critical." —Thomas Bristow, *Transnational Literature*

Books by John Kinsella Include

POETRY

Peripheral Light: Selected Poems
Jam Tree Gully
Drowning in Wheat: Selected Poems
Firebreaks
Insomnia
Metaphysics

FICTION

Morpheus
In the Shade of the Shady Tree (stories)
Hollow Earth
Crow's Breath (stories)
Pushing Back (stories)
Lucida Intervalla

The Mahler Erasures

A Novel

John Kinsella

THE MAHLER ERASURES

A NOVEL

DALKEY ARCHIVE PRESS

Dallas / Dublin

Deep Vellum | Dalkey Archive Press
3000 Commerce Street
Dallas, Texas 75226
www.dalkeyarchive.com

First North American Edition, 2024

Support for this publication has been provided in part by grants from the National Endowment for the Arts, the Texas Commission on the Arts, the City of Dallas Office of Arts and Culture, the Communities Foundation of Texas, and the Addy Foundation.

Paperback ISBN: 9781628974973
Ebook ISBN: 9781628975222

Library of Congress Cataloging-in-Publication Data

Names: Kinsella, John, 1963- author.
Title: The Mahler erasures: a novel / John Kinsella.
Description: First Dalkey Archive edition. | Dallas : Dalkey Archive Press, 2023.
Identifiers: LCCN 2024013119 (print) | LCCN 2024013120 (ebook) |
ISBN 9781628974973 (trade paperback; acid-free paper) |
ISBN 9781628975222 (ebook)

Subjects: LCGFT: Novels. Classification: LCC PR9619.3.K55 M35 2023 (print) |
LCC PR9619.3.K55 (ebook) | DDC 823/.914--dc23/eng/20240423
LC record available at https://lccn.loc.gov/2024013119
LC ebook record available at https://lccn.loc.gov/2024013120

Cover design by Matt Avery
Interior design by Anuj Mathur

Printed in the United States of America

If such inconsistency is a fault, then it's a loveable fault; I find Mahler more touching because of his loveable inconsistencies.

Leonard Bernstein

The Mahler Erasures

John Kinsella

Symphony No. 1

A BULLDOZER DRIVEN for entertainment is an affront to nature in its implication, and likely consequences. A bulldozer driven to alleviate mental and emotional stress is a loose cannon. A bulldozer fuelled and ready to lurch into action is a disaster waiting to happen. In all of this is the idiom of nation, the pedalling of a frontier battered into submission. It is the wren's nest tumbled under the blade, the echidna dismembered, its quills signing off on the travesty of 'development'. If you listen, even from a fair distance, you will hear the rumbling of the CAT engine, carried on the wind—above it, sits a composer of destruction, smug with work ethic but thoroughly enjoying his mission.

Harold is listening, and shuddering. He is the local 'bird kid' to whom all injured creatures, not only birds, are taken. He is projecting forward into his life while feeding an injured juvenile honeyeater with a dropper, when the machine breaks in.

*

In Europe for the first time, he thought he'd escaped hell, without realising yet that he'd entered hell. He was too young then to know home as anything but something you escape from. He was too young to recognise hell in the shining baubles of old Europe set in the crown of modernity. It wasn't so much that he thought he belonged or connected even in part, but that all possibilities were open to him, and that some intrinsic worth in himself would be recognised and acknowledged in a way that it hadn't been in wheatbelt Western Australia, or the Perth of his couple of years at university before it spat him out. A form of personal vanity he couldn't recognise at the time. A small vanity looking for a massive vanity to latch onto.

Harold Lime could barely sing a note, couldn't play an instrument, but had a good ear for music, and had a strong passion for it in all its forms. He wasn't obsessed with one variety of take on music, but just loved music. Though not a punk, he was often at punk music venues, but he was often also seen at classical music concerts at the university and in Perth city, when he could afford it. Money dictated his access.

Raised on a failed farm by his mother and her friend—his 'auntie'—he was happy until he was thirteen, when Mum and Auntie were killed in a car accident, their car sliding on the gravel and rolling, and he was taken on by his mother's brother who had a successful farm, loathed his dead sister, whom he called a 'skinny dyke', and tried to turn him into the male Harold didn't want to be. Harold boarded at a country high-school hostel for the last two years of school before going to one of the residential colleges at the University by the river.

Autosuggestion: I don't belong to any of you, I don't belong to me. I don't identify now with gender, and few other people. I belong nowhere. I am beyond an outsider. You will all consume me and spit out my bones. You all hate me. You will consign me to the nothingness you contrive for those who embarrass you. I have always caused embarrassment. I am less than. I am ineffectual. You will always find ways to accuse me, to relegate me, to prevent me voicing your vanity, selfishness and greed. He really believed this. He reacted to all incoming public information in this way. He was privy to no gossip. Excluded.

Grave's disease is the broody storm that will break and misfire and send the arc between a cathode and anode that are experience and prospect, the hope of refuge in the fierce fire in the sky encounter with events. A trigger makes fury on the road so pull over and breathe, the heart pulsing berserk and the journey from the country down to the city airport to make the leap across the planet to locate a vestige of heritage that might jolly along the internal workings of a mistuned ear. What happened when the concert in the loungeroom wrestled between genteel poverty and old colonial ballrooms, the truth in manacles beneath houses, all that limestone? Could the Graves have come on so early? Such easy fury and putting it down to not fitting in, the excessive bullying. Yes, excessive. Even the girls ganging up to pole you, to mash your shrinking genitals, first year high school pole dancer, you big boy you.

What is nature where will you fit how will the little stories told by family members at Christmas gatherings or collated in the backblocks of memory from earliest tellings as bedtime stories coalesce?—your great-uncle *was*, your great-great-grandmother was orphaned and worked for a mining family in Ballarat; *he* fired his Owen Gun into the jungle as he broke down crossing the mountains on the Trail—he was only seventeen and is still young, if not completely alive. What is this to do with the fastness, the rapidity of events, the futurism that is confronted by Prince Kropotkin in the perfect village you will find? As if the war of Nazism was before time, as if the composer will blast through prejudice, tell his stories in the streets of wheat. He's boiled his brain with ideas, some relatives will say. Easy to mock with cultural gravitas but closer to the truth. What right?

This blast. Heartbeat hits 200 out of synch going off the rails. No sleep but wake up, Brother. Frère Jacques is not waking and the bells are blasting. Those bells calling you to Vienna. To Tübingen. And barely twenty and all that future of instability to encounter, to be remade on railway sleepers. A search for certainty, the orchestra responding. Not recognising Harry in the ear, a voice whispering to wake you from your wide-awake state. Your stunning sleeplessness void of presence. Sleeping wakefulness at full throttle.

*

It is better to be lonely in London than lonely at home, he says to reassure himself. That's young Harold, Old Harold, after a decade in Cambridge later in life, says, Bullshit.

Cambridge. Went there unbelonging. Living on the edges, wandering. The Cam froze over. That summer the Cam was drained. The first winter, that first summer. What was the point? A library card favoured by a drinking companion. Correcting proofs in a basement. Mahler's First at King's. The first time. First of many symphony envisionings.

No way to live, in a basement, shared bathroom. Not student digs, just a basement in a small brick house beyond the golden circle of the university. A rubbish car rental place next door—not a well-known company, just a few barely roadworthy wrecks. And a post office. Always busy. But not too far from the river, and a walk along the banks to Grantchester. And an old dilapidated boathouse with an older hulk inside that came out occasionally and sailed the wrong side of the narrow river. Upset the ducks. Disturbed stoats and pole fishermen. They were always men. The hulk cruised the river looking, looking slow. But Harold saw it and watched it fast, and knew if it came down to it, he'd be preventative. Because he cared and thought if Mahler teaches us anything it's to be protective, value all life, and the cosmos it is set in. At night, he saw the cosmos and thought of code and feathers.

The middle-aged and old men and women who never acknowledge you crossing and touching gloved hands in bargain bins outside secondhand bookshops. Know them all, but never to speak. The words are in the books, if only you can afford them, to be part of the knowledge.

Other Australians. He hears them over the years, but has nothing to do with them, though shopkeepers ask him every day, year in year out, even on Christmas Eve, when he's 'going home'.

A single bar heater that fizzes with the moisture in the basement. In bed with clothes on, moving through the same streets as the young Prynne, the young Hawking. Listening to Mahler on a single-speaker player. Enforced mono. What you learn in the evening out, Harold. The mildew on the walls a busy, rambunctious nature.

He'd hide on VE day, remembering the sickness of the lungs, the rapid heartbeat, the shellshock of earlier incarnations. He'd remember the webbing, the canteen, the burying his rifle in the mud. A Lee Enfield lie. All those inherited tales, all those taking them back to the D Day massings, the Atlantic Wall looking on with curiosity and bewilderment. The agony of hedgerows. As if he was there, as if he was waiting for his number to come up for Vietnam, but that was back home and he was still in school. The fact that Thackeray had written *Vanity Fair* and *Pendennis*, which he still hadn't read, gave him strength. Awake for such long stretches, almost never sleeping, he reassured himself with such facts. But he would read *Pendennis*, he found a copy in a bargain bin, with the page numbering all wrong, a misprint sold as mercy. And the women who shared brandy with him outside Sainsburys in Sidney Street, crofted by Sidney Sussex before being snarled at by a future spokes-couple of the not quite left.

*

Harold had an invention that he wanted to set up in Cambridge, but not to share. A musicological invention—a simple device that you fed Mahler through one end and out the other came Nature. He wanted to share it, but feared it being misused.

*

There is a child. He is an adult now with two children of his own. His own. Nobody owns children. It's best not to possess anything. Own nothing, especially people. Harold hasn't seen the child for thirty years. And never seen the grandchildren. His partner—he was with her six years—only speaks ill of him, he can still feel the words. They hang in the biosphere. She was an actor. What they call a 'minor actor'. Bit parts—working in retail shops to make ends meet. They had drug problems together. They went to counselling. It was 'dysfunctional'. She worked to separate him from the child, an old story. But he wasn't going to go there, to play the gender shit. It was between him & her and there was nothing more to say. Silence is massive.

You overidentify with your grandfather, she said. *Old Harold*, the warman who turned against war. Wouldn't march. Said, Fuck the medals and fuck the marches. I don't want to remember, I've got nothing to learn. I was a kid when I shot people. In the name of the country, the empire. It's like you're channelling him, Harold. You're fucking crackers.

His son—their son—played cricket in the park. He'd taught him that. And the child memorised all his mother's parts and, in fact, whole plays well before he could understand what they meant. He acted as her prompt, as she was cleaning their small flat. She cleaned what had already been cleaned and cleaned it again. She had fixations. Harold made a mess when he was out of it, and she cleaned the mess. And cleaned where there was no mess.

He held a stop and go sign for roadworks on the outskirts of the city. It was occasional work, and he had to do it if he wanted to keep getting the dole. He tried to be sober. He didn't want to hurt anyone by stuffing up—it wasn't just because he didn't want to get caught. He took his role seriously. He didn't even drink with the fellas after work. He just did his job, stiffly. Alone. One time a truck ignored his sign and kept going and ploughed into a slow-moving inspection vehicle, writing it off. Nobody was seriously injured. There was an investigation but plenty of witness said they saw not only the red stop sign, but Harold wildly gesticulating to the truck driver to slow down slow down to STOP STOP!

*

He was crossing Magdalene early one morning before things really got going, and found an injured duck pressed against a Quayside pillar. He picked it up, as its head lolled, and cradled it in his jacket. It shat on him and he said to it, At least you're alive. It annoyed him people had been walking past, ignoring the duck. But then a woman holding the hand of a little girl walked close, slowed, and said, Is it okay? She had an Australian accent. That was usually enough to drive him away, but he said, I will take it to the Duck Lady. The Duck Lady? asked the woman. Yes, she lives in one of the narrowboats just up from the Lock, near the swimming pool. In the red one with potplants and planter boxes all over the roof. She looks after sick ducks. And then the little girl, whose greyish hair was aflame in the sunlight which had just broken through the thick indelible pencilled cloud, started singing,

> All along the backwater,
> Through the rushes tall,
> Ducks are a-dabbling,
> Up tails all!

That's from Ratty! she said, bobbing up and down. I hope the ducky is okay. It will be, said Harold, as the duck nuzzled its beak into his armpit. I can tell. *Wind in the Willows* is cool, said the girl. She likes *Wind in the Willows*, said the woman, the mother, embarrassed and proud. Well, we hope the duck is okay. Come on Linda, she said to the girl, arms extending as the girl went up on tiptoes to see the duck and the woman started walking towards town. It will be okay. It will be fine. And then he heard the women saying to the child, He had an Australian accent, could you tell? No, not really Mum, said the girl in Cambridge English with a touch of Strine.

Then people were pushing and shoving as bikes raced passed and a bus crammed tourists into students and townsfolk and the bubbling of Cambridge got started suddenly, in earnest.

*

When they first met she'd looked like Grace Slick in the 1967 American Bandstand clip of 'White Rabbit'. Gothic. She used to mime to the song. Harold didn't look like any of the blokes in Jefferson Airplane, having dreadlocks and glasses, but uncool glasses with a string so when he nodded off they didn't hit the ground. She'd come from a fundamentalist Christian background, but that wasn't why she wore a huge cross on a long string around her neck—in fact, it was because she'd dramatically turned against the congregation which she was known at particularly bitter moments to call The Coven. What they did in Jesus's name was unforgivable, she said. They wouldn't know Jesus if they bumped into him in the supermarket. The both bonded over 'morning maniac music', listening to the Woodstock appearance and pulling cones as the sun rose through an open suburban window, both naked. That night she worked backstage on the *Accidental Death of An Anarchist.* She wasn't a great fan of Mahler, and that was a problem for him, though he realised this was a ridiculous thing to worry about.

*

He saw the woman and the *ducks-are a-dabbling* girl again crossing the bridge, and he could see they were being pestered by someone in a thickly padded hooded jacket. The woman was saying, Please leave us alone, I don't want to talk. Sorry, I don't care if you're *also* an Australian, I have no nation and want none. As he shuffled by, Harold restrained the urge to grab the hooded figure, and smiled at the girl who recognised him. 'Look, Mum, it's the duck man who took the sick duck to the duck lady on the red narrowboat!' Harold tapped the peak of his hat, and slightly bowed, wondering why as he did so, and the hooded figure broke away and merged into the flow of students and bikes rushing into town.

Are you okay? he asked the woman.

Yes, yes, she said sort of irritably. Harold couldn't really tell because he'd forgotten how to read people in any meaningful way.

Was he bothering you?

He? Who, Pat . . . Patricia? No, just irritating me. She wants me to join the Australian and New Zealand Social Group. They have get-togethers and Fosters on AFL grand finals, Australia Day, or when there are Ashes cricket matches on or some rightwing Prime Minister is visiting and crawling up to the aristocracy and their gimps . . . you know, bowing to the colonial overlords, and other travesties. It makes me ill.

I understand, said Harold. Neither of them was going to mention that the other was 'Australian'.

Then the girl piped up: 'Mum says that there are always spiky people around to make a story happen.'

The woman patted the girl on the head and said, Well, something like that. And then turning to Harold she said, Well, have a good day—looks like the sun might break through low in the sky. Then as she stepped off, she flicked her eyes towards the tower of St John's New Court, and said, Cambridge is so implicated in its own wonder. I detest the smugness. Those sleeping rough just outside the travel shop near Sainsburys will be sorting out their sleeping stuff at the moment. Wonder how many of the privileged will put something in their paper cups? Yesterday, I saw Salman Rushdie walking past them, getting lost in the crowd. I don't know if he threw them any money or not. I'd like to think he handed something over, hand to hand, making physical contact.

They still use candles in the Magdalene dining hall, said Harold. He was conscious his nose was dripping, though turned and shuffled off before wiping it with the back of his fingerless-mittened hand.

*

The next time Harold encountered them was on Jesus Green near Jesus Ditch and the woman was trying to coax the girl down from a tree. Harold wondered how on earth the girl had managed to scale the tree in the first place because it had a long smooth trunk and no lower branches. The girl was yelling down, I won't come down I won't—the world is nasty to me and I don't like it! How is it nasty? the mother was imploring. Because you said there'd be blue sky today and it's just nasty old grey again. Always nasty old grey and cold and wet! When summer comes we'll go to Strawberry Fair on Midsummer Common, you'll like that. Just like last year. It was sunny and warm, remember. Yes, but it was muddy because it had poured and poured the day before and there was yucky cow manure mixed in! The girl drew out one of the 'poured's as long as she could. And then she reached into her puffer jacket with one hand, holding on to a branch with the other, and threw a sodden tissue down at her mother. Embarrassed, her mother leant down and picked up the tissue and, about to stuff it in her own pocket, glanced quickly around while achieving that supramundane feat of keeping a nervous eye on her child, picking up the tissue without really looking at it, and, scanning the environs, chanced upon Harold. Further, she could see Harold was worried she'd think he was stalking her, but from the way he was sitting (in the distance), and his attempts at concentrating on his reading task (a biography of Mahler read in poor, dappled light) and listening to the flow of water in the ditch, she didn't really think this for a moment. The woman calls out to him, She's upset because we've had to leave our flat and stay in temporary accommodation—a European wasp infestation in the roof.

Hello! it's you, Harold called back with self-conscious artifice if not disingenuousness. He wanted to add, is the girl okay? but said, I often have to move and it's always a strain, especially if you have to move back to the same place again.

Where do you live, duckman? yelled—spat the girl.

Why, I live in a basement.

What are you reading?

It's a biography of a great composer called Mahler. It's a very big book—he wrote nine and a bit symphonies.

A bit?

Yes, he never finished the tenth.

Why?

If you come down I'll tell you and, if it's okay with your mum, show you the book. His voice was growing hoarse from shouting.

Before the mother had had time to process all this, the girl had shimmied down and was studying the pages of the biography over the shoulder of Harold, perched on a rock.

The pages are damp, said the girl.

Yes, as you know, there was soft rain a little while ago. But the book is compelling and I can't put it down and sometimes I forget I am outdoors.

How can you do that, said the girl. Listen to the birds—they don't sound like that from inside. But wasps do—buzz buzz, chatter chatter against the ceiling, in the walls! What does Mahler's music sound like? She said 'Mahler' perfectly.

*

Hunt sabbing. No characters even loosely based, they met the night before. The horns are resoundingly loud, the hounds hither and tither, the accents break out in parody of literature's direst moments. That's what we're dealing with. He listened to her, saying, I don't like cruelty. Nor do we—and we use every non-violent means we have available. I don't want to be part of any group, but I do want to let the foxes run free, he said.

*

The Red Forest. Massive boars, lopsided horses, dogs in attack packs. Truths. Visitors to the region look down on the plant, bubbling death into the sea, back into the mountains. He only dreamt awake, never when asleep. He only dreamt in daylight. He said, I am being called. They are trying to decommission me. Seagulls are walking the water of the first-generation Magnox storage pond. They are processing the banality.

*

Harold believed he was cryptobiotic. He was alive, but his life was barely detectable. She and her daughter had noticed him. This mattered to him. His frostbitten fingers and toes were repairing, and his drought-addled memories were filling out again. He realised those who'd reprocessed him, mixing him with vitreous glass at high temperature and turning him into a capsule that could be stored in an indifferent town like Cambridge, had gambled he'd stay relatively inert until 'retired'. But they were wrong. And he was going to act.

*

Harold lay in bed bursting for a piss. It was cold and he didn't want to get up. He had a container he pissed in stashed under the bed but it was full. He'd have to go out of the basement, up the uncarpeted stairs, to the ground floor bathroom. He tried to drift back into sleep but his insides ached. He was getting a dose of prostatitis, which would make the coming days hell, and he had no pain killers left. He thought of just letting the piss go and enjoying the momentary warmth. But there was nowhere to dry his sheets and blankets, and he had an aversion to such stenches. That old congress. It was all coming back, those imperfect words in something resembling an acceptable order. I am a product of bullshit, he thought and laughed just enough to drive a spot of piss out. No holding back now, so he leapt out of bed, held the open crotch of his pyjama pants together, and shuffled—no, strode—to the door, the stairs, and to the bathroom which was fortunately unoccupied. As he pissed hard and long, he looked out through the crack of the open window at the first cold light and could see the sky was clear. It's going to be a good day. The prostatitis seemed to have dispersed with the release, and he felt this to be a good omen. No going back to bed, as he usually would, just lying there and thinking it makes sense to get through till lunch, but back to his room, and dressed, and reading the Mahler biography under the lamp. Then out, outside with the blue tits and coal tits, the robins and other birds of the almost budding hedges and shrubs. He listened to the 1st—only the 1st at the moment, he assured himself, he qualified and justified. Only the first. All things in their proper order. Have to start at the beginning again. Right back to the symphonic poem. To Titan. To two parts. This is the second part of my life, this is a new beginning. And I don't even want it to be my life. I hand my life over—the second part won't be my own, and the two parts won't balance. Lopsided, but I am not sure which way. The horses galloping, the wolves roaming the streets of Cambridge and attacking the scientists whose vivisections are hidden by lunching.

*

Do you know Maupassant's story, 'Claire de Lune'?

Yes, the misogynist sees the folly of his ways—has an insight into the feminine that supports his world. And nature flows through him and he is illuminated, understanding there are things beyond him. It is the perfect story.

Yes, I wish you'd behave like that epiphany was with you when you interact with me, she said. She wasn't looking at him, she was studying lines for a Brecht play. Which one was it? She was twenty-two, he was twenty-four.

Well, if the Abbé can see, I guess there's hope for me he said, chopping the potato into cubes. And I prefer moonlight to daylight.

And she stopped work, looked up, and said, Yes, you are an evening person. You are nicest in the evenings.

Yes, I like the owlet nightjars and tawny frogmouths and owls.

*

Harold was fifteen and alone in the bush. Not lost, just alone. In the swathes of leaves of York gums and jam trees, weebills were hopping about, very vocal. There were also gerygones and thornbills making community, and a mistletoe bird—a female—was singing nearby. Harold remembered the old man who used to shoot the tiny and exquisite mistletoe birds, saying he was helping the jam trees out, the same ones he'd bulldoze next year. I connect with so many stories I haven't and will never read, he thought. And yet, here I am, in the bush, in a story. Not lost, just alone.

And then he heard a vehicle coming down the bush track, and thought, Not only am I not alone, I face a certain death if I stay here. For a nanosecond he amused himself with archaic modes of speech and thought about syntax. Then, unable to help himself, he pulled one of the dope plants up by the roots, heads of sinsemilla oozing resin, and ran, trying his hardest not to damage the vegetation as he plunged through it in search of a deep aloneness that wasn't death. And as he ran, a Nancy Drew novel fell from his jacket. Even then he knew it had been ghost-written. He looked at his watch and it said 2 P.M. but the sun was straight overhead. Something was out of kilter in the universe, and the shadows were grabbing at his ankles like tentacles. And he hadn't even had his first joint of the day. And this wonderful shit had to be dried and cured, though he knew he'd be bunging it in an open oven and drying it quick—it was so good it could afford to lose a little of its efficacy. He heard older men yelling, Someone's fucking ripped us off! His heart vomited onto the ground and the more carnivorously inclined birds dived on it.

*

I am not the same as I was then, he insisted. Connecting me to that past will tell you nothing.

*

When she came to the door with her friend, he was hesitant. Outside of the landlord and one other tenant, he'd never invited anyone into his basement room, or any of the other rooms he'd occupied in Cambridge. He let them in, and registered they felt awkward, looking around for somewhere to sit. He offered his reading chair to her, and the desk chair to her friend, and sat on the bed. The stranger was maybe five years older than the woman, making her maybe the same age as him, though he felt older, much older. He was forty-five. He thought of himself as sixty-five.

The women were looking at the bits and pieces on his desk. The Mahler biography, an edition of Kant, the collected poems of Gerard Manley Hopkins, a selected poems of Judith Wright, a collection of Oodgeroo's. You like poetry? the stranger asked, though it was self-evident. He didn't think it strange that she asked. Yes, I do. And then the other woman, the one with the girl, said, And you collect feathers? There are some amazing feathers here. Yes, he said, I just pick them up when I'm walking. Shuffling. He wasn't going to shuffle any more. He was going to get fit, like he did when he reached puberty—always getting fit, always trying to build muscle. Your daughter is at school? Yes, the woman laughed. Then, seeing that her laugh had perplexed him, she added, She didn't want to go to school today, she wanted to help plan how to save the foxes. The stranger, with a certain vehemence, said, She'd be better off doing that than going to school! Harold shifted on the bed, glad that he hadn't pissed in it a few days back, thought the squeaking springs made him wonder why he'd allowed them to meet him here, in his retreat, his only place away from the world. Already he was planning to leave, to move on. It wouldn't work now. He wanted to be in a room with woods close by, with marshland and waterbirds. It was, after all, why he'd come to the edge of the fens. To hear the 1st in such a place.

Symphony No. 2: The Resurrection

IN HIS FIRST year at primary school, Harold was tormented and tortured by students and teacher. To expiate his inability to move on rather than excoriate the horror from his past, she made him recount it to her as she helped him move into his new 'digs'. He loathed the way she called the room near the woods 'digs', but he didn't loathe her. Sitting with her, perched on the bed, which hadn't been made, cradling a cuppa made with his electric jug, he confessed.

In Bata Scout shoes
I stood in the bin
and knew there was only me and it,
knew the bin for the receptacle
it was, with curdling milk
and pencil shavings
and snotty tissues
and paper not screwed

up very tight because small
hands found it difficult.

In school uniform the socks
are long and reach up almost
to scuffy knees and Bata Scouts
are shiny shoes if kept
in good order and in the heel
is a compass that shows true north
and sits under a flap in the inner sole.
It can be crushed. Who said,
Design flaw? Just in case,
the makers provided you with
a lemon-juice secret writing kit
so you could always get a message out.

Punishment is the rubbish bin
or standing on the desk
and trying not to fall fall fall
as teacher reads to the semi-circle,
reads Dick & Dora but you've read
ahead of yourself, through all the *Wide*
Range Readers read them at home
and not in time with the class
like singing where the hand moves
and reading and singing in your
'broken home'. Teacher tells you
in the rubbish bin facing the corner
long before the hand-held
horror movie long before

and tells the semi-circle
and the desks with Cuisenaire rods
all colour codes you read back,
you over-reading interpolator
you, that your home is *broken*
and so are you, *so are you.*

So to, so to vomit warm milk
in bottles left in crates in the sun
on the verandahs that shade none,
your schoolcases under the seats,
the toilets too dangerous
to stay in long, the ball
that comes into range
an explosive device
and chalk on the bitumen
a code you're learning fast
like the flag and 'Let's Join In'
coming through the grey eye
of the PA speaker over the blackboard
which the headmaster barks orders from
and you know if you see him, it will hurt.

There are others and you will
befriend and be befriended
or stand in the rubbish bin,
isolation unit. Your time-machine
head doesn't have permission
to be age-inappropriate
and your peers

will write reports
in their first big letters,
their adventures
with the alphabet.

Play is healthy
play is in the afternoons
play is like God in your secular school
Meccano is not play
and your father leaving
his Meccano for you to play with
brass shiny steam engine and thousands
of tiny nuts and bolts and spanners to fit
and his giant jigsaw puzzles of ocean scenes
and schooners all white fitting into each other
are not play. Children do not play
in 'broken homes'. Heads down,
time for a nap.

It is hot and always
around the time the time
of your birthday your birth
day when school starts
in the heat, the heat
that burns and peels
that inscribes your future
that plays with your skin
to be cut out to not grow
back the same.

And when Mum's friend
comes to live in your house
where the bush still grows
and the river runs but also
runs into a dead end,
a swampy end with snakes,
where big fish come up from the sea
and the river bends and joins
another river which runs all
the way up near the farm
where cockatoos and parrots
play games too and they fall
in an enfilade of feathers
and there is blood
other than your own
knocked down at school
fallen from the bin,
toppling over. Your 'broken
home' remade but not in the image
of teacher who comes back
to claim you the next year,
no breaking away: 'Don't think
two women make a house
don't think it's not breaking
and is not broken worse'.

And Mum's friend comes
with her old car
her old car 'Louisa'
her old grey car

which is a 'classic now'
but would incite seven- and eight-
year-olds to pummel you mercilessly
for its being old and broken (though it was
so well-kept) and even the kids
whose fathers beat them senseless
drunk in asbestos boxes
where the government (THE GOVERNMENT)
herded them, 'State Housing', but their families
black-eyed unbroken, were one step up
from your home which was happy
was happy with puppet plays
and tools and books
and it was broken
as the pollution
in the bottom of the rubbish bin
which you had to empty into the big outdoor bins
when you stepped out at the end of the day
for using running writing
for doing long division
in the world of two plus two.

The edges of the school.
The western side beyond
the pine-tree divide,
cordon sanitaire
and why wonder
wonder why you write
the line, the wild crossing?

The Swamp.
Short-necked tortoise, so rare.
Where you can't go but do,
where poems will embed
and flowers
when the rare orchids
have been 'made gone'.
Modong and swamp paperbark,
scarlet runner and swamp-hens.
And late in school, on the demarcation line
of high school, you will go deep in with friends
and the approval of the school to make a movie
of pith-hat wearing explorers fighting off
the 'natives'. Bamboo spears. Yelling.
What do those boys, long gone
from your life's narrative,
you long gone from theirs,
think about this now?
Consequences.
Imprint.
Embedding.
Swamp of the Gums,
drained by garden bores,
entangled by garden escapees.
Swans wilting. Dick and Dora.
Fluff and Nip. Fast-food wrappers
floating on the black-blue waters.
A lost brother leaves school to explore
the swamp without damage,
without prejudice, and is cut by cane

to the bone. Remember. Remember.
Peaks and troughs. Zig-zag line.
Write 'wigwams and mountains'.

Already this war talk,
these games you can join in:
shooting and falling at a distance.
The hand a pistol
the arm a rifle
and teacher seems
unruffled by all this dying.
Permission granted.
A rubbish-bin triumph.

In the bin for my sin. The sin bin panel
vans are yet to appear,
but they will. They
surely will.

Lost younger brother
will appear on the rolls
and in class photos.
His Grade One to your
Grade Three. Pathfinder.
And he with redbacks
nurtured in his school desk,
under the lid for inspection.
The headmaster uses his name
through the one-eyed grey box
up high over the blackboard.

At first we walk home together,
our initials painted on our cases
by our signwriter-in-the-family,
and then we don't. When
I am surrounded by bikes
and corralled into my future,
he is down at the swamp
looking at insects.
And so he should.
And so he should.

But we play. My rules.
Wars. The rules: I win.
To win somewhere,
fall-guy brother.
And he will look out for me
when I fuck up
so often later: the dealers
wanting whatever they can scrape
from me. Into the rubbish bin
of my body.

A rifle shot takes down a 28 parrot.
How to rewrite so many bloodied feathers?
Looking up into the salmon gum,
up past the embodiment
of rainbow and all fairy tales
and war stories you feed on.
A sheep is slaughtered
and its contents are rubbish.

In the 'broken home'
many animals come
to shelter. A kangaroo.
Birds. Dogs. Reptiles.
Insects. Paradise Lost
is a murmur from the bedroom.
The fall the fall the fall.
Odysseus speaks back from a cassette.
What choice. War and journey?
The forces who would
break hospitality,
the making of a new Australia,
the social modelling of school,
Let's join in, let the fun begin.

There are friends.
One farts so bad, teacher
says, Someone needs
to see the doctor.

There are friends.
English boys from the hostel.
Their mothers leave
and go with Greek guys.
More than one? You can't find
any of them on the internet
now. Says something.
Says, Home that was.

There are friends
tossed together in the tempest
of new highways and banksia
cones falling and burrowing
to the centre of the earth.

I am Gigantor.
I am Prince Planet.
I am Fantasia.
There are friends.
My lost brother.

The house. The house
of mother and father,
both worked long
hours for. The broken house
healed together. Through
the floorboards a coin falls,
beneath the house you crawl
on your belly to explore
the centre of the world.

Soldiers from America came in the war.
When the ships of the fleet return
the officers are in living rooms
and sailors in the streets
of the port, the city.
War. And the advice
after another beating
is 'join the forces'. You don't want to end

up in the trash-can
of existence, son.

But the communist
who has been years
in China will come
and rearrange
the hierarchy. Yet
that's three years off
and the kangaroo hops
across the buffalo grass
of the back lawn.
Goldfish swim
in the submerged
concrete trough.
Tropes. Recurring.
What is different?
Why are shell-casings
being collected?
Reload load your own.
Arsenal. Fairy!
is not how you see
yourself. But already you are,
spreading wildfire even
in winter, a cold wind
off the Antarctic.
Fairy! like smuts rising
from the woodstove.
Hand-me-downs
from cousins.

Fluff. Nip. Word belongs to picture.
Huey Duey and Louie. Uncle Scrooge.
Money Bags. Show Bags. Dad comes
down down down from the mines
UP NORTH and buys dozens
and dozens of showbags.
The ghost train. The freak
in the halflight doesn't frighten
the product of a 'broken home'.
Substitute age-appropriate talk
even though you didn't talk like that.
Dictionary was liberation.
Fairy floss all around the rubbish bin
but none in. Off-target. Pink and blue
world of spun sugar. Army surplus
jacket. Pieces of iron ore
gifts in your flighty pockets,
weighing down to be man
in household run by two women.
Dick and Dora and Jack and May
caught a magic carpet to Mandalay.
The compass in your shoe
will show the way.
You can come too,
my lost brother.

A nulla nulla. A boomerang.
Pictures of a mia mia. That is
all we learn of whose land
we're on. Interpolation.

No, of 'who came before'. After
that, 'primitive' will cascade
down through life and all
walking will be in the dust of.
But you are waiting. Never left
never leaving always there.
Not hard to hear. Not hard
to see. That scratchy ink
on the white page. Artefacts
handed round the class, touched,
grabbed, passed on quickly.
A nulla nulla. A boomerang.

Workshop. Nip at my heels.
Dad's tools left behind. Orderly
wreckage. I make. Catapult.
Go-kart. Intricate small cities.
Rifle stocks. Animal houses.
Blood and lead. I hover
over the grey slurry,
inhale deeply. Remember
first hearing the words:
'environmental disaster'. 1970.
Red Badge of Courage
and first school bank account.
Migrant integration. We,
we of the old colonial.
We of the diaspora.
We of the death rays.
We of *Lost in Space.*

We of the rubbish bin,
the landfill on Heirisson Island
already chock-a-block
and a visit to the tip
with Mum's friend, my other parent,
my father while my father is away
away UP NORTH making a new
family, my mum's friend my friend
to the tip where she keeps an eye out
for anything useful. Opportunism.
I can spell it. I deploy it. Not military,
just enthusiastic. Like trying
to save the dusky minor
fallen from the nest with a dropper
and mushed-up Weetbix, or the lamb
from the farm butting the teat on the Coke bottle,
the warm white Coke bottle: lamb and kangaroo
and dog on the buffalo grass.
I am Gigantor.
I am Prince Planet.
Teacher cannot tell me otherwise.
I cannot see her as I look into the corner
from the rubbish bin, crying dry
in this drought-land. Hot as hell.

*

It's shit to keep that stuff stuck inside you, she said. I was saying to J. (who introduced them), that you have a lot of shit stored up inside.

Changing the subject, he asked, How is her child? Is she still angry about school?

The school says they don't know what to do with her. Good sign, I say.

And is she still being harassed by the person in the hooded jacket? He wanted to add, By that *Australian*, but held it back.

Yes. I said she should go to the police.

But she won't.

Of course not.

That's a good sign, he said.

*

Who claims the big music of death? he asked her.

Do you have any religion?

No, but I did once. Growing up. And I thought I had a vocation. I have a cousin who converted to Islam, and another cousin who is a Zen Buddhist. My ex- was a pagan. I had a boyfriend when I left school who had been an Anglican altar boy. I read Aldous Huxley's *The Perennial Philosophy*. I have only ever been to one funeral and it was that of my grandfather who was also called Harold. I came from generation on generation of Harolds. I often don't feel myself. '*Hic Harold rex interfectus est . . .*'

The Bayeux Tapestry?

Yes, my grandfather had one eye—the other was shot out during the Second World War. He was in his forties when he fought at Tobruk. A rat. I am searching out origins—the truth of whorl, the eye. Do you know the Charles Chauvel film, *The Rats of Tobruk*? The American critics rated it dire. My grandfather was in Camden in 1944. Not in Africa. He was on the set. An extra. If you look at the Wiki entry, it cites the *New York Times* critic saying of its release there in 1951 that it was 'eighty-five minutes of crawling agony'. And you know the Harold hit in the eye biz is contested. Ask the scholars here in Cambridge. They might condescend to enlighten you. I don't like computers, but I sometimes use one in the town library. Anyway, why are you here?

I am here to get away from there.

Sounds reasonable. By *there* I guess you mean Australia.

Yes and no. I was the target of a recruitment campaign.

A drug mule? A terrorist operative?

Don't be glib. I speak to you because you are not glib. Because I trust you.

I am glib. I am lost. I have impure thoughts, though I cast them down down. I am not the man I used to be. I am no man. I do not like men. I have lived other people's lives and live everyone's death. I have tried to catch mice in humane traps to reduce plague, to transfer them away from the focal point, their concentration. I have tried to catch and release Asian House Shrews so they don't stink up the shack on the edge of the beach, the monsoon making the long drawn-out waves murky. To the bemusement of locals. I detest banks and yet a bank in Perth Western Australia holds my last will and testament, and a surprise for those I've named as heirs. I have nothing material to leave, but the will will be contested. You can trust me. Who tried to recruit you? Did they succeed? No, actually, I don't want to know. It's not relevant. It's been so long since I've talked at length with anyone that I am getting carried away. Sorry.

*

I don't like this 'coming out of your shell' stuff. I want to go back to my shuffling off my mortal coil. Just eking out my time.

*

These collections in this town. These archives of extinction. Humans, animal, plants. All in there. The record of their pillaging, of their science. I will liberate them all. Can I recruit her to this? No, she doesn't want to be recruited. She will decide herself. She will suggest it to me, I can feel it. And all her sab friends. They will come to the *party*. I do not go to parties, I do not follow parties, I celebrate no parties.

*

In jail, the only blokes who would take any notice of what I said and not torment me were Noongar guys. In their hell, they still found time to nurse me back into purpose, a desire to live. One of the guys hummed Beethoven's 'Minuet in G' to me and said, I was taught that in school on a scholarship. I was going to be the one in our family that got inside their system and undid it. It caught me out and locked me up.

*

People don't walk around me anymore, they walk into

me—they want to impact me, send me off my line. The clamour of bells distracts them and I pass by as quick as I can manage, which is not rapidly. The voices are real. Somebody is singing in the street. In the hall down the road an amateur choir practices three nights a week. They are not a religious choir. That is unusual, especially here. Sometimes I go to King's to hear Evensong. The recognise me at the door and I don't have to pay. Those glorious voices are not celestial to me. They are anchored to the earth. They get stuck in the vaulting.

*

Stopping the arms manufacturers—that's where we have to start.

*

Those stories I wrote when I was young against racism I can now see were racist, or could be read as such. All I cared about was resisting racism, and yet I fell into literary tropes and clichés. It's because I didn't have the tools to leave my learning, though I had inklings, and there was enough there to allow the self-critique to begin. It's a slow process, unlearning.

Fire weather and the trauma of point of view. They suffer, we suffer, I suffer, you suffer. Heat and high winds and dry grass and idiots flicking lit cigarette butts out car windows. Country life. You. You. You. We know better. And that's not taking the moral higher ground—fire rushes up the hill, searching for space, oxygen, the sky.

*

The trade delegation, the arms manufacturers, and a visit from the Prime Minister of Humpty Dumpty Land. Bailing him up in the dunnies of OzHouse, you, Harold, told him some homefront truths. Without emphasis, without emphatic language, without explanation marks. He was shocked that you knew so much about military hardware, especially of the historical varieties, and didn't want a selfie, though he said you could take one of him in front of the urinals. So, you think you're going to resurrect an economy, thrive after you've pillaged the country by manufacturing devices of misery, torture and death. Selective with your clientele. Let's trace the journey of the AK47. Come with me to the British Museum, loving empire as you do. Visited many times? Urbane. Don't you love the poets who will cluster around your benefits, the shrapnel, like they do in Canada. Internationalise it. Accept the money and say nothing. That's the spirit, like the glowingly *white* poet from the fillet's eye of Australia, doing his song-cycle oompah-band imitation-celebration of fairground rides and treats on sticks. No, this is not satire, I don't know how to do that and despise it anyway. Prime Minister, you will blast us into the top ten of death merchants. It's one occasion when the cliché is the best metaphor. It's quite literal though, isn't it? Not really figurative. You and your love of statues, your narrow spectrum of equality, your hashtag in internet military profits. Not me, mate, not me. I'm back to my hovel, back to the basement, back to my spaceship, leaving the station and becoming shooting stars as it enters your atmosphere. Love your security, love your detail. Nice suits. Good weapons. Homemade? Through the airport scanners? The diplomatic bag? Visiting the depressed hacker. Takeaway ambassadors? You and the genius finding a way through the telephone lines? Broadband unlimited? Heat traces of joggers around Pine Gap. That's the spirit, the spirit of Humpydumpty land?

*

The hollowing winds, the easterlies, the fire winds the death winds of a wheatbelt childhood. The woosh, the glow like sunrise as you struggle out of sleep into windows of fire, the roar. Wind and fire violently arguing and feeding and betraying and lusting. Guilt is your last register. Then pain. But that's different.

*

I don't care if you think it's 'similar' in any way. It can't be. It is not a package, it is not literature, it is not autobiography—it is disgust, response, rejection. And also embracing the hope and release and connection. None of you can take that away. And if I quote all of Hardy's Tess herein, it will be as much mine as his, ours, yours. Really, it's Tess's and I asked and she gave her permission. But I don't need to tell you that. I won't say why. I can actually be trusted, I can. Here, sans quote marks but with a font of its own: On an evening in the latter part of May a middle-aged man was walking homeward from Shaston to the village of Marlott, in the adjoining Vale of

Blakemore, or Blackmoor. The pair of legs that carried him were rickety, and there was a bias in his gait which inclined him somewhat to the left of a straight line. He occasionally gave a smart nod, as if in confirmation of some opinion, though he was not thinking of anything in particular. That was a relation of mine. Somebody traced him for me. I can only do exposition.

*

I don't blame my parents for who I am though they both disagreed as to who I was. Mother remains, but father is coming back. I know. But 'Auntie' was my real father. I know. And Uncle said *he* was my punishment. For what?

*

She calls me a tyrant, says I am obsessed with my own originality. Where to go, how to process. The codger upstairs has complained about my talking to myself in the bathroom, in the corridor. He says it's, Unsettling. Old bastard. Thinks he's a cut above the colonial in the basement. What was he in his college life? A tutor of English. He still does the odd supervision—bright young things come to his door after letting themselves in through the front door without so much as a knock. He says that I talk to myself. Well, he struts around spouting King Lear and Hamlet and Everyman like he's the only one who knows what's going on. Wanker.

*

We all have to live somewhere and now I am living alone by the fens. Alone? Well, they both visit me here. The sab woman and the woman with the girl. I am a project for the sab woman, and that's okay. I don't mind. I actually look forward to her visits. She slept over one night last week—on the floor wrapped in a sleeping bag. There's almost no furniture here. I did not offer her my bed. Why would I? She played me Kate Bush's violin song & dance on her phone. I said, That's death's violin. Mahler knew all violins—their many characters and moods . . . infinite, really. Why don't you own a phone or a computer? she asked. Why would I? I said. I said. I said. Am I real to you? she asked. I said: I am not real to me, so how can you be? She finished the bottle of wine by herself. Sometimes I piss the bed, I said.

*

There was a small legacy. Not a lot. How could there be a lot, given the circumstances, the demands on their capital? And what would you expect. If you want, and desire, it is toxic. Death's money. How does one come to be where one is not wanted? Where there's a system of tracking down, confronting, dragging away, deleting. I go to hear a poetry reading in Brixton and there's energy and home and sharing and doormen say, Be careful man, the bastards are on the prowl looking for marks. Eager to sling slang arrows outside your patois. They'll delete you man, just like they'd delete us but we're rooted in the soil of their conquests. We are the barnacles on Walter Raleigh's over-enthusiastic vessel. We are the poems from The Tower, the sugar in their racist tea.

So, I wake in the morning in clean sheets and a sweet-smelling room, tucked in tight in a single bed that doesn't squeak when I move. I hear morning prayers coming from outside, over traffic. I am still in London, somewhere. I like where I am. I stagger up in search of a toilet, the pain sharp and urgent. There's a boy and a girl in school uniforms walking towards me, laughing. Hey man, says the boy, a crest on his jacket. You okay, Man? says the girl, a different crest on her shirt pocket. Hi, I say, and my shuffle gets worse. You looking for the toilet? asks the boy. It's down the stairs, to the left. Don't trip on the stairs, says the girl, but light-like, with no nastiness. They are nice kids. I negotiate the stairs and can hear myself sigh with relief as the piss leaves the bladder. I embarrass myself—I've lost the art of manners. I wash scrupulously, dry my hands on a white towel with pink lettering that says, Guest. I go out, think about going back upstairs and making my bed. There's an older man and woman sitting at a table—I can see them subtly looking at me, glancing at me, through an open door. The kitchen. She looks away, then turns around decisively, pokes her through the door and says, Coffee, love?

I have seen you! I say to the man eating his breakfast. The kids have gone to school. Yes, I am an actor, he said. You might have seen me on television. I am sorry, I say, with a little embarrassment I find disturbing as I hate television, I don't watch a lot of television. And then the woman—his wife?—says, He's most recently been on an episode of *Midsomer Murders*. I have seen an episode of that, I say, But that was years and years ago back in Australia. Yes, the woman says quickly, You didn't see many non-white faces on *Midsomer* back then! On British television in general! he said. And they laughed. And Harold struggled to get hold of the narrative and understand his own need somehow to indicate the non-white status of the household. He wanted to consider the prayer, the blazers, the skin colour, the context of his being discovered talking to himself after the music had stopped at the club in the morning. What time? 1 A.M. maybe. But none of these people were there, he was sure. So how?

Thanks for everything, he said. I need to go back to the fens. He shuffles towards the door, bumping a small table in the corridor. I am confused, he wanted to say but couldn't. And then the man is leaning in front of him and opening the door, and as Harold slowly breaks into the London day, all of it too fast for him, the man hands him two twenty-quid notes and says, This should get you home. I will pay you back, stumbles Harold. Not necessary, but if you want. Push it through the letterbox in an envelope, or don't. It doesn't matter. You have been a good guest.

*

He had overlanded from Australia. Well, from Java. And then he'd leapt across Pakistan, Afghanistan and Iran, and ended up in Turkey. And then another slow journey to The Channel. Grandfather Harold has gone to the Levant via Gibraltar. Troop ships. Leaving port was where all emotion resided, arrivals where deadening.

*

Tea. In Cambridge, those who taught the poisonous politics of tea drank it in copious quantities, knowing the qualities and quality of a leaf. The labour. The profiteering. The trade equations.

*

The sea. In the fens, it's what he thought about, coming up The Wash, spilling out over the banks, the dykes, ditches, canals. The ocean rising into his home, so far inland. As the Inland Sea was his imagination, was his version of internal exile. The unbelonging. Soon, I will be 20,000 leagues beneath, and all Cambridge's crazy sciences will be with me, casting unseeable shadows at such a great depth, the sea's surfacing touching the sky, eating into space and being eaten in return. Under the sea I will be wrong as I am on this dry world that's only dry because the pumps keep going, the windmills turning. I have no status and no desire to rights here or there. I am a dry drunk. I am in a wet town as a dry. I have no right to comment on the most brutal overlord of his or her or its own community, and yet I must state what I feel is right or wrong or I cede my humanity. I have no status and own nothing and want nothing other than my humanity. A right I believe I have even where the light can't get through, but where the light once was. Because they've done this to the world, doesn't mean I want a bit of the crumbs of disaster, a bit of the sludge might be more accurate, but I still want what I am to be me. I am I was only a path to possession and ownership—but I possess nothing but the space of my own body and the space of my thoughts. That is all I am—owning nothing. Just isness.

*

Australia's efforts to homogenise fortunately failed. As it will fail here, too. He said this as the churchbells rang out over the still astonishingly white village. The dead will not be restless with the change, he said, They will rest easier when it comes. They get to see the folly of the ways of their times, and the exceptions to the rules they lived under. Rules they will know they should have broken. When the sea disinters and spreads the atoms of who we are throughout and over, emulsifying. When the resurrection—for want of another word—comes. Not the reckoning, not the tribulation, not the harrowing, not the apocalypse which is already on us in its various manifestations and semantics, but the resurrection. Together we will become aware of the damage we have done—all of us, even the righteous.

You do go on, the sab said, because she liked to hold the floor and what she was on about was vital. Which it was—he supported it, and blew horns from behind the hedges, buzzingly alive. She just didn't concern herself with her own whiteness—she was for the animals, for whom racism was not an issue, was it. Speciesism? Only from humans, Old Man (as she'd come to call him because he didn't or couldn't or wouldn't or whatever 'fuck', not that she liked that kind of intrusion anyway). Gathering with the other sabs, it was like a mass action though they were small in number. The whole orchestra there, and she as conductor. The fox was the note they were tracking and yet protecting. The squelchy ground, the wet grass, the drystone walls, the agonised yews and beech trees, even a small straggling elm. A stayer, against the odds. Spotted woodpeckers marking out soft parts of a WHICH tree. And there the planted conifers. And there hornbeam and ash. And there a fallow deer. And there coppiced anomalies. And there the four-wheeler and shotguns. And there rifles. And there red jackets. And there hounds. And horses. And there P. J. Harvey as alternative as woodland management and gamekeepers. And there the fantasy novelists and there the city audience. And there Dungeons and Dragons. And there and there. The finale, the resurrection. And there and there and there.

Between the First and Second Movements: vacant contemplation?

He had been in a town which shut down as a funeral procession marched by, but he couldn't recall where or when. It might be in the future. It couldn't be his own funeral as there'd be no mourners. When his grandfather died there'd been a gathering, but in the cemetery. There'd been no wake, no celebration of his life. Just a gathering of silence outside the appropriate words. What were those words?

*

Yes, I had friends at school—three across twelve years. Approximately one ever four years—they didn't overlap as friends, though I knew two at any given time. The last friend became a scientist and big game hunter. He and *eye* not only didn't see eye to eye, but he replaced the eyes of his victims with glass. In my final year of high school, he decided to study what he called 'the art of taxidermy'. After that, I swore there'd be no more friends for me. Since then, I've had associates and associations and I had a partner who had many friends, many hundreds of friends, all equally important to her as she was to them. She was in the theatre. She is quite famous now, I think—being in movies. I went to one of her movies three years ago in the Cambridge Arts Cinema. I heard students and dons saying to each other, Isn't she stunning. A stunner in the fashion of those enslaved women of the Pre-Raphaelite Brotherhood? Like that? We actually had a poster of Millais's *Ophelia* floating . . . floating over our bedhead. When we were first together the bed was springs and cardboard. Now she could buy the original, I guess. She searched me out in Cambridge once—I hid in my basement. Or a loft. Wherever I was, smelling of urine. I would say to her, I love the life in Ophelia's face—she's not dead, not remotely. We read it all wrong. That stimulated her, my saying such things. But in the end, in the long run, after all was said and done, I couldn't reciprocate. Not really. Not forever. Though I think I could love. I do. But she didn't believe me, not ultimately, not in the end. When all was said. And done. With. One of my relatives said to me, smirking, She has done so well for herself. She has.

*

When they locked me up. In various rooms, in cells, in recreation areas. Bars, reinforced glass, the wiry lines of graph paper inside the clarity. I traced the crossroads with my finger over and over till I had located myself, my upper half—all below brick and wooden framed. I heard the beatings we are meant to deny hearing—the kickings given by the authorities in their various uniforms. And the deals done by some of those interned to make life easier for themselves—behind the scenes, with their confidantes the guards. Them. They kick hardest when the kicking is to be done. And to stand in front of the judge and say nothing—just looking filthy and maintain a lack of clarity in the gaze, staring straight through him or her, which bothers more than most crimes. The hand of the law is a very egotistical thing. A lot invested in stage, the throne, the gavel. I have seen the killings covered up in the lock-up, but like the time I saw a Thylacine in the wheatbelt of Western Australia, I speak and write it and no one takes any notice. As if it's not evidence, as if it's just illustration. But I write it and say it and nothing is done, no cold case investigation of the crimes of the state by so-called corruption watchdogs. So why write? Why bother? But no, each step managed, each piss taken, each line read in the Mahler biography, each annotation made to a phrase in a symphony, each wave of the baton caught in the mind's eye a writing—listening to the sound of one's own breathing, one's own voice. Reading it. I am only my experience and my processing. I am unoriginal, I am limited, I am less than minor, I am irrelevant. I forget the names of the authors of the great works I read and they will stay forgotten. Only Mahler speaks to me now, as himself, not as a name on a spine on a jacket on a screen, which I occasionally glimpse at in the Cambridge Town Library. But rarely. But I am, to contradict myself, an index. A form of index.

*

I have been asked to read some of my poems at an event this Wednesday night. Will you come along? I haven't read in public in many years. I don't really write poems anymore. Though I have some in my head I haven't written out. I might do so. I published a couple of chapbooks—small booklets—of poetry when I first came to Cambridge, and they were read and discussed by a handful of people. I see the publisher in the streets every now and again, but he knows I don't want to talk so leaves me be. But as I was standing outside Heffers looking through the window he saw me and came up and tapped me on the shoulder and apologised for disturbing me and said, We are having a twentieth anniversary celebration of X books, and it would be wonderful if you would read. I know you don't write or don't want to publish, but those works of yours are still discussed. I felt ashamed, and said, I have been out and about more than usual of late. I have two friends. Can they come? Of course, he said, clearly delighted. And then I got ahead of myself because something of the old spark, the embarrassing old spark, the shameful urge towards express-ing myself in public, poked its claw through and said, I have some new poems in my head I have been reworking for years and maybe the time is right to copy them out—I could read a couple, or recite a couple . . . ? I was confused. He said yes, told me the details, asked if I was still living in the same place which was meaningless because I had lived in so many places since our social days so many years ago. He then turned and was about to leave when he said, I am sorry that the reading is being held in a university building, but as you know many of our poets are of the university. I was glad he didn't say something like, I don't want you to feel uncomfortable—detestable word. It's okay, I said. I have been out and about more than usual of late. I have been listening to Mahler's 2nd a lot.

*

Cracking hardy is a loose cannon on the plains of masculinity down where the red dust is vacuum-cleaned into bunkers. Macherey seems to mean what he's saying, rather than merely trying to create an effect. Not that effects can't guide us through the smog, but if smog is the discovery, as well, then nothing much is gained. And I detest the word 'discovery'. Billabong. Wooden finches. All of these issues in the poem I am trying to retrieve at present. I hear it, but on the page it twists and turns and changes. But reciting from memory incarcerates the poem even more than the field, the enclosure of the page which is really no enclosure if you stare at it long enough. I need no hypertext to show me the way—another guide through the smog to smog. Cracking hardy. I learnt what that meant in the changerooms of high school. It morphs, adapts, goes with the colonial that reinvents itself to suit. Character is never really different, characters rarely different—just their choices and behaviours, occasionally cross-wiring. I can't believe I differ from anyone else, not really. I can believe what I experience and feel and suffer and enjoy and respond to and receive and what informs my responses is different. But I know this is wrong thinking and I know why. I read books and I see one character of many manifestations, wherever the character comes from, whatever the cultural coordinates. This is not about people, this is about the artifice of literature. Entering into that negotiation with a book-reading public conditioned by capitalism. I cannot publish again. I will handwrite my poems and circulate a few copies. Does that mean I want to be read, that I am a character of my own devising making poems without identifiable characters therein, without a single personal pronoun? All allusion to a life, and illusion of non-participation, non-culpability? I would rather piss in the bottle but the bottle is full and I can't, I know I can't, not really, piss my bed. But it's time for a cuppa and that compels one upwards. Green tea fills the tummy. The appropriation, the glib fucking irony. And yet, it is why I drink it, and for the effect. The last thing left after so many years, the last shreds of addiction. Between us, down here before I have to leave, I say it. I play the Mahler so quiet, how can the old bastard upstairs complain about it. And yet he does, identifying the symphony, the conductor, the recording, and the old needle in the groove music machine. I think it's the record player he hates most. He can barely pay his rent but has an iPhone.

Symphony No. 3

Brassy beginnings. The callout. This comes later—we are going back, listening 'live', in situ at a remove, layering in. Attention! Harold is musing over a Ducky Double icy pole from Peters, early 70s, after school. It is melting and he can't eat it fast enough. He cannot remember pleasure or pain, just the frustration. It is hot. Very hot. He is gathering the materials of skin cancers and a loathing for nostalgia. Too many loathings spread across the entire orchestra, struggling with its hierarchies. Did Ducky Doubles become Twin Poles, now also lost to heavy strings? To a growing awareness of the *sell* of evolution. It would be a decade at least before he discovers mutual aid, the full joys of a solo cello.

A church in the fens has nothing to do with God—nor does a family chapel on a bush corner of a farm in wheatbelt Western Australia. But Harold had been told as a young boy that Nature was God. He asks now if it was God then but not now, or if it's God now and was never so back then, or never ever. As if a theologian might own emphasis.

He reads 'Stocks Recover'. On the verge of annihilation with the Doomsday Clock sitting close to final moments, stocks recover. Optimism on the floor. As Hannah Arendt noted of imperialism, the bourgeoisie who had left political power in the hands of the state knew suddenly that their wealth could only be increased to massive proportions by seizing political power themselves. In the Nazis they sought a path and were ultimately 'liquidated'. Harold processes and reprocesses this again and again as he thinks of his impending visit with the *shes* to the shores of the Sea of Ireland, to Cambria of the glass bricks. The sab woman and the woman with the girl (who is letting her girl stay over at a friend's for a few nights as it's school holidays as the girls' friend's mother is also a friend of the woman). He wonders why he can't cope with names. He was moving out of the basement but has decided—been allowed—to stay for a few months longer. The man upstairs has tried to engage him in conversation about Mahler, and then referred to the filthy rings on the bath. But I never wash, says Harold.

*

When I went to school (one of my schools . . . this echo is not an accusation or a wistful remembering, but a broadening of the set of possibilities and consequences) on the bus—almost an hour's ride—I stewed over the aggressive and intrusive and braggart conversations of the other passengers. Kids from the same school. They bragged about shooting and scramble bike riding and looking at porno. I ignored them and they thumped me in the arm—the permanent bruise. But on my own, against my own sense of things, I imitated them. I was monstrous without the social environment to diffuse it. Without the banter that would allow me to grow, move on, abandon the insensitivity. I rode mad into the wind, hacking up ants' nests, screaming lines of Keats into the melting. The searing easterlies.

Outside windows it's always better where the eye reaches clarinet and flute, or piccolo mockery of what's being seen, or maybe a pale imitation, this out of place templating? Brazen trombone, pulling all towards it, vacuuming then blowing out the stars that are up there if you train hard enough to see beyond the blue sheen of day. What creeps in from *Scheherazade*? What fantastical renderings from different zones to make the empires extend throughout the body. What hijackings of DNA? What obsessions with DNA in the first place? What eugenics of musicology? Can a kid on a bus to a school which will be his doom think this? Is this why he will write essays on interpolation into Homeric poetry in his first year of university so many cymbal clashes down the track?

*

You think that a refusal to make decisions of 'relevance' leaves me worthless and ash outside the town of burning decisions, of ultimatums, of cryptic chambers and big-noting decision-making that leaves them saying, He's a bastard, but you've got to admit he gets things done. Like concentrating agricultural poisons administration in the big property colonial heartlands, fostering tragicomedies of vengeance in rural cinemas where the chances are the showpony jokes will take root, where the irony of the pc reversal to have your cake and eat it too will flourish. All at sea, in the complete experimental, all hungry for sea cows and knowledge. Discovery. A name that claims and challenges like Enterprise. Frightening at the expense of. The ligaments failing and injections of cortisone. Do they follow the trail from grass to serum to needle? This molecular mix-up.

*

Reactor dragons. He saw them. They all saw then, flourishing out of the decommissioning. I have seen them before, said Harold. Over the fresh reactors they are vibrantly aggressive. They fly through bodies whereas these collide. And I have seen them out in the arid places, where the ground is being disturbed. Monitors with immensity, with codes to ancientness the collectors and surveyors and 'environmental advisory services' seek to put in their very small place. A ratio of maybe one to ten thousand. This bit put aside (for now), and the rest open for St Georging.

*

I was walking by the river. The Swan River. *Derbarl Yerrigan*—the Noongar name I don't use in conversation because I do not wish to appropriate it. I was thinking the thoughts of others, thinking the thoughts of kids in the back of station wagons crossing the freeway watching the swan and sailing ship on the lights of the mocking brewery.

Even then we kids knew it was true, that 'true' wasn't even a word to be used. We knew when we heard of the rainbow serpent that all of it was near and around and under us, and the 'wadjella' adults our parents and guardians wouldn't believe or couldn't hear or see. I was walking along the banks of the river where the rich want their views clear through to the incipient skyscrapers, the big money, the mining money that made the city. Made. I too visited the W. A. Mining Club as a guest of . . . just because I wasn't sure how to be impolite. Like other characters like echoes of myself as I am an echo of other writings. I see myself there, feeling ill as the Captains of Industry discuss the testicles of their pedigree American Pit Bull. I am walking and I am seeing the poisoners poisoning trees with religious glee. I am crossing a pond on a small wooden bridge on reclaimed land and a family of crested grebes, feather-full, float from under the bridge, beaks tucked in feathers over the shoulders, emitting high-pitched whistles. I am with her, arm in arm, and we are watching them and she is discussing a production of *Hedda Gabbler* forthcoming, funded by the oil and gas industry. Her brother is on a platform off Karratha on the Northwest Shelf. Her father is in the Miner's Club, planning a meeting with his mistress who he has just given a small red Mercedes sports which sticks to the road like glue even as she bends round Mount's Bay Road at twice the speed limit. Daddy says he gave you money for the kitty and you spent it on pot and sherry, she said to him, as we talked of Judge Brack. I didn't have a leg to stand on, and said so looking at the seagulls in patches all standing on one leg. There's a lot of research into the single-leg standing of birds. Then a

Caspian Tern flew past, pointed winged, and we wandered to the river's edge where on the concrete retaining wall of the grand reclamation eight darters—snake necks—perched drying their wings, ink dripping into the upset river. Would he be back there years later musing over corellas swinging from paperbarks by their beaks, excavating the grassed areas for roots, discussing the extinction of Major Mitchell's cockatoos in the central wheatbelt, the decline of barnacles on condemned jetties closed off to the public, swallow nesting zones, the quick emergence from underneath looking into the changes wrought by imperialists, the island made, the Narrows, the lawyers finding ways around claims that might upset the balance of inequality. Choppers passing over, the Crown Casino tower block head-butting the inversion layer, the Scarp hollowed away, a platform for houses and building companies. And soon, soon, the recreational shooters blasting away in the reserves, the parks. Is this him in the future, escaped from the basement, the loft, the mildewed rooms of Cambridge? Is this him with the woman with the girl returned to Australia, to start anew? No. That won't happen. And the 'sab lady' (his mind grabs whatever is there, out of date as it might be . . . but who does he say it to? who can it offend? and he barely exchanges a word with her anyway, just following her lead . . . in balaclava and smoky coloured clothes, blending into nothingness . . . he refuses camouflage, refuses the militarisation . . . he cannot cope with the ultimate ironies, the hypocrisies) is drawing him deeper into the resistance. Sometimes, sleeping on the floor near him—as near as she can get, she hears him muttering, 'Albert Tucker's Ibis in Swamp Albert Tucker's Ibis in

Swamp Albert Tucker's Ibis in Swamp'. She listens as long as she can, before growing restless and twisting in her sleeping bag and disturbing him into a deathly silence.

*

All those years of not fitting in. He is not remotely social-adjusted, he heard. Socially. Adjusted. Remotely. Not. Won't mix with other children, sits alone at parties, plays with chemicals which can only be anti-social. Older, those kids who ostracised play with chemicals at parties and it's cool. So he indulges ten times for them then and plunges and is cast out out out! The social organism. Where are all the people—the other people—in the narratives. The. Narratives. Other. People?

He is buying fruit. He needs vitamin C or he will get rickets. A woman came up to him shuffling through the streets, imperfect on the cobbles, and said that. Men give him a wide birth. He is buying fruit and the person at the counter yells out, You're 10p short. What have you got there in your pocket? Do you have 10p? The person is yelling and people are looking. To leave without the fruit, but leave with the shame. It must make for rickets.

Never stole a thing. Never a lolly. And yet when another kid did so from the deli when he was down in the city visiting, visiting, *parents* discussing things with someone, and yet when another kid stole a lolly from right behind the counter, walking around and sticking his hand under the glass—maybe ten lollies, grabbing a handful of strawberry jellies and fluorescent yellow bananas and cobbers that smash your teeth and never unstick not till you lose all the teeth or die—and grabbing and running and you, Harold, me, I, Harold, standing there in astonishment and watching watching and saying nothing and being accused and somehow a father who was gone is suddenly there and two belts are entwined and welting the bare buttocks where the big jobs come out welting and sucking tears back into the eyes so extreme are the sobs. Why? Why, people. People. Why?

He said to a friend who was *made* to have him—Harold—as a friend. He said, I am looking and listening and touching everything now so when I am old I will remember everything that has gone. That sounds stupid, said the other child. Let's go and kick the footie down the park. We can do that, said Harold. And Harold kicked the footie a few times at odd angles and then sat down to consider the occasion, the soft grass with yellow sand showing through, the black lawn beetles rising and falling, the diamonds of backyard showing through asbestos fences lining the par.

The plastic curves of swings swinging though there was a light breeze. The smell and taste of something electric in the air—the transformer that had exploded three nights ago and blacked out the suburb. I don't really live here, said Harold, though he was attending school there now. It is not my home though I like to remember. He could not remember the compulsory friend's name, he could not remember what he or she—likely a he?—was wearing. But could remember the impression the sandshoes of the person left in the patchy grass—all scuffed and dug up with enthusiastic kicking. And there was a dragonfly hovering though it wasn't the dragonfly season. He remembered to remember it. The yelp of a Labrador puppy enclosed in a chicken pen in a backyard, visible through a broken diamond. Five A.M. precisely and time to be heading 'home'. The other child lived nearby. They would sign off on the friendship with their parents' approval. That Harold *is* a strange child. A loner. That's actually how they spoke—it's not a convention. So say all of us.

*

Blazon brazen trumpet fanfare collapse into wonder of overegged universe the finches' beaks shape-shifting on the islands and the Beagle collecting barnacles on its hull. Amniotic as a desalination plant, solo against the pit is corrosion or leading up the garden path. Cutting through St John's, over the indeterminate waters, keeping head down. Confidence trick. Why do images of Swiss Pocket knives and spiral stairs and a street choir in Vienna come to mind?

Whose fruit-cutting adventures are these segueing or nudging in? Cross-reference every photo taken by a tourist of other tourists, locals a blur they can't make out on developing, or illuminating. Magic 8-ball working overtime, rugged up against expectations of powdery snow, red dust, the clashes, the triangle apostrophes, *the clamour* of little bells. Sleighs, maybe. Snow queens? Ratatatat. Reading Joseph Roth again as between-the-lines history. Percussion is truth. Percussion is confrontation. Percussion is glory with the rug pulled out. From beneath. Its. It's.

Ratatat ratata RATATATAT! Blazon trumpet, blazon heraldry inlay class mobility stifled.

But it becomes dislocated—you pause in listening though the music goes on. What key have you missed, what key bit. Blazon trumpet blazon, bullroarer. To fill in the marri blossom with red-tailed black cockatoos, they're enticing and mournful call beyond instruments of commercial construction. But then the bus pulls into town and a Nazi swastika has been Roundup-ed into a lawn. The only green lawn in town. They won't recall that when they don't want to. You are down in the city at your first orchestral concert. It is Mahler. It is large and massive and creation is sucked into its vacuum. Programme notes direct you to creativity rather than imperial cultural trajectory. In there, an enclave of hope. And winning the history prize there's that book on Hitler—history, condemning to prevent it ever happening again, but there it is in the lawn. And decades later you'll hear of it happening again, brought to your attention by a friend. A flourish and the side of the recording is finished. Complete. Where it leaves you, beaten by fascists, picked up by the actress because she has pity. Her father's sympathies nudging, but wary of the Eureka stockade incarnation of a flag because the Southern Cross is raised against his developments. The boss and his workers share so much, but so little.

*

God-shaped hole? I am nothing. I am not he nor he nor it. I am nothing. I claim nothing and want only the space I occupy without acknowledgement. I claim no seconds of your time, your precious self-time. Give it to the ducks, the swans, the owls, the magpies. Give it to the space left by flight, the digested ground left by earthworms. They name themselves and define themselves and I can't say. I just cannot. I am not.

*

Do you remember the disquisition on the hunters at Wolfsegg in Thomas Bernhard's *Extinction*?

Yes.

Well, it's true what he says about hunters and fascism. In Australia they bully their way into power and all too often—always? am I being too placating, too cautious?—align with far-right social policies. They see themselves as being close to the earth and reasonable and the most sensible of all people. Pig-shooting women's groups consider themselves at the forefront of tackling gender inequality and bigotry, while subscribing to the codes of control. I do not implicate Aboriginal hunters in this, though it doesn't necessarily mean there aren't individuals who subscribe to the broader imperialist mechanisms of hunting imperialism. But they would be the exceptions, and not a cultural normative. In fact, the imperialist hunters while claiming certain kinships with Indigenous hunting societies, in fact do all they can to undo rights and autonomy. Colonial hunters are always liars. They see themselves as noble people who understand the earth. I know all this because until I was a young man—well into my teens—I too was a hunter. But I struggled with my masculinity and the killing was contrary to everything I aspired to. My uncle expected it of me, and I too readily complied.

We need people like you, who have seen the light, said the sab woman. Converted.

I am no convert—I knew it was wrong when I did it.

Inside knowledge is useful.

Well, it's pretty straight forward—the hunter will think you're ignorant and they *know*. They will dissemble. They will say things like they're doing it to 'control vermin', when in fact they are doing to fulfil their bloodlust. I have, working way out on the edges of the semi-arid zone, heard multiple men talk of how if it was legal they wouldn't mind hunting a few people. Not casual talk, but pumped up pissed aggro shit. Incontrovertible. So much care spent looking after their rifles. Oiled and cleaned and the smells of walnut and gunmetal a perfume of power.

What do you make of hunting in Maryse Condé's *Segu*?

It is a fiction. A historical fiction. History of trauma moves sideways as you read it. I don't wish to talk anymore. Can you please leave. I would like to sleep in my room alone tonight. I don't want you sleeping on the floor, talking to me so I can't sleep.

*

I do not read anymore. I have stopped reading. I only listen to Mahler. Now the third, which says nothing to me about my life, my surroundings. I do not know what nature is. Is it the weeds growing where the herbicide has missed around the slaughter house? Is it the packet marked vegan next to the boiled-down animal dessert sitting next to it on the refrigerated shelf? I read the labels. I eat nothing now. I drink water, and water filtered and purified in ways people can't know: at least people not in the water supply industry—and even then, so often unthinking or uninterested. I describe a bird to the woman's daughter who is looking at the ducks near the punts, as a spruiker spins a deal card on his hand. It's their thing—the card spinning. The bridge is busy, and stories crossover, briefly entwine. Some of the least aggressive looking are predators, hunting for footnotes or appendices or even full main paragraphs for their own stories, to create out of seeing others. I feel them drilling my head because I shuffle, because I talk to the woman and girl. The girl is holding a book, a copy of *The Wind in the Willows*. She won't let go of it, says her mother.

*

What kind of name is that?

What do you mean?

Where does it come from.

I don't identify.

You must know the origin of your name.

It is irrelevant to this moment, our engagement in the here and now. What you say to me, how I respond has nothing to do with the origin of my name.

To me it does.

Then I will have to leave this shop. I will not shop here again.

Touchy, aren't we!

*

I hear reports. I wouldn't say 'from home', but it's where I came from. I hear of fires caused by tourists lighting campfires to have a bush experience with snaggers. Ignoring the signs—NO FIRE! And then a spark, then out of control, and thousands of hectares of bush destroyed. The 'tourist' might be a visitor from the city. Fire is something they always feel they can control. All of them, all of the theys. The wind picking up, 'conditions changing'. I hear only because houses have been lost, razed. Sheds and fences. And livestock. Outdoors. Camping. Mildew on the ceiling. Erasmus with the rivercold in his bones. An echo from elsewhere?

*

What makes you recoil when you are a ten-year-old and a kid in your class starts distributing nationalist-socialist propaganda and calls you a 'black-loving bum-diseased communist'? When their old man drops them off at school with the iron cross with an Australia flag inside and 'Fuck OFF We're Full' stickers on the back window of the ute? What makes you say to critics when you're older and trying it out, saying that rural Western Australia has a lot of far-right-wingers terrorising the community. Stereotypes? Clichés? The audience sick of hearing the same old same old? Was that her friend saying that? He was her biggest booster—don't hold her back, she's on her way to America. You're such an old stick in the mud. Exact expression. Stuck on all that shit no one is interested in outside the CWA hall. As highschool crashed into reality, shot up the bush, you were without sexuality as far as other students were concerned. Even the lesbian who came out in Year 11 was given space because she spouted more racist screeds than anyone else, and not as a smokescreen but because she believed them to the core of her being. Her father was a member of the organisation. That's a mistake campaigners for gay rights have often made from the streets of cities—right-wing rural towns, even religious ones, often have enclaves of tolerance for homosexuality as long as it can be compartmentalised and as long as the general politics of the subjects are not lefty greenie redrags. You try to explain that to some but are misunderstood and, having no sexuality, no identity, are condemned, too. It's easy condemning, isn't it. The blood of a dead animal washes away so many prejudices and even the sex-haters in their factory churches can find a place for the killers of vermin. Vermin being an indeterminate variable. And that's the bloody rub. He's such a bore, her mates said. He's lacking in . . . personality. He's suppressed gay he's suppressed hetero he's just drab. Drab. Drab. Who is being discussed, do you know him or her? This is a tough part of the script to memorise because it's so unpalatable. He is sexless. He doesn't even have the guts to become a monk. That's because he doesn't believe in God. Godless and sexless. And doesn't believe in 'race'? And doesn't believe in killing. And doesn't believe in himself. Loser. Seriously, you've heard all of that, haven't you? So limp, so lame, lacking in literary depth. Where is the texture of fur rubbed the wrong way, the dried blood quills of short fur of rabbits, the cottontail, the abrasive rub of dried and drought-scorched bone? Where is the torn skin of climbing rockfaces, the itch of pollen disturbed or grit in the bathers at the beach, the thrill of sunlight on your prick getting changed. You prickless godless lacklustre waste of space. God-shaped hole.

*

Harold enjoyed grouting though was indifferent to the end results. But preparing the surface and spreading the grout and placing and inserting the tiny ceramic tiles and making it regular and neutral appealed, comforted. It is enough, he said. When he forgot to pick up his pay his partner rang her dad because she was so at a loss. Leave him, her father said, the bloke is an idiot. My daughter deserves better than being with a eunuch idiot. Her father was a potent man with a nine-inch prick. He told everyone this. He worked in inches rather than centimetres because it sounding 'more imposing', more rigid.

*

Tempo di Menuetto. Movements II–VI. Mahler has nothing to do with. These undercurrents of the New Fascism. The sneaking through of Wagnerian overtones. Zero! Such shuffling in the basement, hovering in the loft so light from abstention, a wraith with rags on. Always that urine smell. I. You. We. He, Harold.

Which instrument leads us down the garden path, lures us in? All jolly openings are Little Red Riding hoodwinks. Why do you always moan and whinge and carry on about the 'negatives' of the world, Hal? Distant aunties and uncles called him Hal. Some of his cousins called him Harry. Occasionally, for a reason he could never ascertain, his twin-girl first cousins on his father's side called him Henry and giggled. They spied on him in the outside dunny somewhere but he couldn't recall where. The opening of the second movement was a Saturday-afternoon technicolour movie marathon with happy hunters going out in leather pants to blow away the witches, the ghouls, the Communists, the threats. He hadn't liked sports much, though he did enjoy skipping and basketball. Why do strings soar so happily? he asked a music teacher. Settles the audience for the gravitas or maybe trouble to come. But all nature, even the hideous destructive bits, is to be celebrated, she said. Another music teacher was an ex-army bandmaster and he liked passages with pace, with a bit of a gallop. Or a sensible march. That's all true. Honestly.

The landlord has intruded or let one of the other boarders in—there's an Air Wick freshener automatic spray gadget stuck in a double adapter with my record player plugged alongside it. The gadget is spraying sickly scent into the air. The room smells like a morgue now. Out out!

I confront the landlord who points down the corridor to the scholar. I knock on his door. He is drunk. I lean against his doorframe and tell him how so often where I come from the rain evaporates before it hits the ground. He says, And where again was it you come from?

Nowhere in particular—well, a place where the rain evaporates before it hits the ground. And if it does find the ground it steams back up, but not far, as it vanishes in the liminal zone.

Stones have been known to move . . . and, you know, *trees to speak.*

You know where I come from—that's because of open-cut mines. A bloody business.

*

My daughter is so *femme*, she said to Harold as they sat on a bench outside the Round Church. On the ground, to the left of Harold, sat a half-full bottle of cider in dappled shade. He no longer drank booze, but felt tempted to pick it up and drain the bottle. Because of the risk of catching something. He has spent his life both paranoid of germs and enticed by them. My daughter is so *femme* and I have absolutely no interest in 'girly' things. When I was a child I refused to wear dresses and played with matchbox cars, never dolls. But it's not really about denial, or what I wouldn't play with, because I would have played with them if people hadn't tried to force me to 'enjoy' them. It was a choice of resistance, which was more annoying to the adults because I was otherwise a 'good girl', and was polite and diligent and did my work. The girls at school liked me though I wasn't interested in their frippery—but there was always another 'serious' girl who wasn't really interested in being girly. What bugged me—excuse the expression—was that I wasn't allowed to express an interest in 'nature' outside it being pretty or lovely. And I am not talking about 'tooth & claw', I am talking about anything outside the illustrative, anything outside what can be converted into parable or fairy tale. Nature was allowed to be cautionary or illustrate what was deemed appropriate behaviour, but not as a thing in itself. I kept a little pot of dirt on my bedhead once because I liked to look at it through a magnifying glass and my mother poured it out saying the flower had died because I'd forgotten to water it. I said, There was no flower in there—I was studying the dirt. And she said, Don't be so silly . . . and messy, dear! Oooo-wwwww-ha! Sorry, that yarn just got away! I guess I am more tired than I know. The girl had me up at five this morning—she said she saw a ghost. It floated above her and told her the answers to today's arithmetic test. Maybe that means she got up and studied. Or maybe she just saw a ghost. I have seen ghosts, said Harold. And they both watched a magpie approach before it flew up into the shadows.

*

Though I have denied it till now, or if I haven't I can't

remember—that is denied it to you, in recent times, in the here and now—though I might have denied it, or said otherwise, I *do* have a sister . . . what some term a 'half-sister'. She was the child of my father and the child of an exotic dancer. My father denied ever seeing my sister's mother at work, though my mother insists he bought her with a fifty in her g-string. That was the only occasion my mother ever referred to my sister's mother. My sister—Joanne—lived with us for six months when I was seven and she was eleven. She set the backyard on fire and only my dam survived, dry as it was at the time. She told me things so rude I thought them impossible. She forced me to urinate in front of her. On the first flickers of the flames but I didn't have enough piss to extinguish them and they ran away from us. Joanne laughed a lot and said you won't go far with *that* tinkle, Harry. She called me Harry and I hated it. I liked her, really, and missed her when she went. I didn't see her again for fifteen years. One night when a guy of my own age I was obsessed with but who found me ridiculous took me out on the town—I only went because I was in awe of him and didn't know what else to do—we went to a brothel. The guy bought the woman for me and I was shunted into a room and recognised Joanne straight away. We laughed about the fire and told tales of our dad, neither of us having seen him for years. We talked about grandfather Harold and his war wounds. As I was leaving, she asked if my tinkle had grown. And I said, I still couldn't put out any fire you lit with it. She slapped me on my back and said, Have a good life, Harry!

*

I have a new girlfriend, she said.

That's good.

It's good for the girl—she likes Anna and behaves for her. She's a feisty young one—difficult to control sometimes. Anna has authority, at least for the time being.

I don't trust authority.

That's easy to say.

Yes, it comes across as glib, doesn't it? Here am I, alone, without responsibility for another. What have I got to say about it?

That's just self-indulgent.

Yes, it is. I sometimes find it hard even to speak.

Would you like to meet Anna?

Not really. But I don't mind either. If I come across the three of you in the street I am happy to say hello—just not to make a special occasion of it.

I understand. I won't push you. You mean if it happens natural-like?

Yes, natural-like.

*

They deny the Nazis are in the wheatbelt because their own politics don't stand out and they are not targeted. They don't register anything beyond the 'odd bad egg', their own politics demi-polite on the surface—conservative—but virulent behind closed doors. They see themselves as patriotic, reliable, hard-working, nation-building, and fair. All else is ratbaggery. The fascists don't target them because they are aware they are the net of silence that allows their own extremities to prosper. That's why, said Harold. Why was he arguing with the woman's harasser? Why was he sitting in a coffee shop drinking a pot of green tea? He loathed coffee shops, he loathed chit-chat, he loathed expatriates, and he loathed harassment. And here he was, a lightning rod. They deny as the kids sing a song of sixpence they utter anti-Semitic stereotypes to all & sundry without knowing the Euro art they praise as real culture is so often Jewish in origin and character and generosity and intensity and questioning and bleakness and wonder and joy and partying good fun and everything. They hate the idea of 'Asians' and go to Bali with their partying parents and love to rip off vendors who they tell everyone when they get back are rip-off merchants but didn't pull the batik over their eyes. The mystery of their existences, of their stockpiling bows and arrows and crossbows with splayed dartheads and lumps of four-be-two with nails stickin' out of 'em. This is the fucking reality, and why would I want to remember the signalings the chorales of kids wishing death upon difference. You have no idea. No idea. The flag on the back of the backpack is a deathsign. This is not appropriation of others' trauma this is trauma imposed for sympathy or empathy it's the kid sexually abused in the school toilets because he's a poofter. And Harold said, Gay marriage is a great thing as far as marriage goes, but it will save none of the kids who like me fall prey to the normative. You are bitter, he hears, And you shouldn't say that stuff. Seriously—in the exquisite range of the uncracked voices as he parks himself in King's or the St John's school choir he hears all the unsaids the unknowns the innocence institutions and their minions and their manipulators and their disciples have fed upon. Who is to say who is to say? Watch your diet, look after yourself, watch your mental health, don't live in realms of mildew sporing your lungs and thinking of higher things, celestial voices, the intactness of all drawn into the score into the performance. Harold likes to think they will all be fine, all their best interests looked after. Left alone to be as they are. But his own experience tells him it's almost impossible, even if it's in ways they themselves cannot know. You are bitter because of your own experiences, Harold, It has made you a lonely removed sterile and characterless old man before your time. Your distrust, your fatalism, your search for an ethereal you predispose towards failure.

*

Why would you befriend my harasser?

I don't befriend people?

You befriended me and my daughter.

Did I? Anyway, I just got in a conversation to find out what makes your harasser tick.

It makes me feel very uncomfortable.

I don't know what to say. Are you playing games? I mean, I don't really know you. Does my friend sleep on the floor next to your bed? I thought you were working together on animal rights stuff—sab stuff.

Why are you asking and why does it matter? We don't sleep together because I don't sleep with other people any more. I am sexless.

That doesn't make me trust you.

I don't enjoy conversations like this—it reminds me of why I don't like speech or company.

*

The river. No, it's upriver. The 'Avon' they call it. Near the bridge—just west—salt-scarred banks, limpid waters after summer rains have drained through . . . out of the heat, the dry, a big burst that brings a tint of green the farmers kill off with poisons because green at the 'wrong time of year' does their heads in. Green on bare hills and plains is a reminder of generational footings years back when the clearing was done at a back-breaking cost and the renamings to fit the dales and plains of a green England and Wales and sometimes bits of Scotland and Ireland were put into play. The river west of the bridge before it curves south, past the flood area where the town was first despite warnings from Whadjuk people that it would be washed away then moved to higher ground. There you are and I am, looking down at a white-faced heron always in the same place always looking north as the reflective surface diminishes. Always looking north, back to the escaping convict Moondyne Joe who is weaving his way through the bush all the way to the Scarp where he will look down from granites over the coastal plain and possible plunder to take back to his hideout in a gully surrounded by tall marri trees, but here, now, where the heron is and also remnant flooded gums and insects in small plumes and a dragonfly, a lone dragonfly where and when there might have been many. But as I look and find company in the skerricks of nature I remember in this exile that I cling to in the unrolling of a trained river devastated by farmer ecology by remaking in one's own colonial image and paucity of imagination in this metaphorless and symbolless watercolour with the water lowering and thickening with fewer waterholes to keep going with the long dry run till winter the heron is suddenly facing south its beak on the horizontal an event horizon looking into the far bank over the algae the insect plumes the dragonfly crossing its spirit-level bubble of truth its speech held back its rage against such massive encroachment facing south as if Zaruthustra comes down from the communications masts overlooking the town on its hill vantagepoint the jam trees wreathing the ascent to a God that can't be sure of consistent reception. This first movement colliding with the song & games, the Moondyne Festival convict frivolities, the sausage sizzle in the main street of memory banks. Facing south, defiantly.

*

What does it say?

What does he say?

I slept. An eternity.

Pan is back—a nuisance, a harasser.

Do we have more to go on? Maybe a gender ID?

No, nothing. Just a tune, a corny song. *Kookaburra Sits in the Old Gum Tree* like he owns it.

The copyright of the pit, of commercial immensity.

We had it forced on us over the eye of the classroom

loudspeaker. We sang a tune to the queen, and old man kookaburra. Gender balance at the end of the 60s.

Everything comes at a cost, as the protocapitalists instilled.
Indeed. What does nature have to say? About. It?

*

Six notions of massive deception. Singing for his supper, Harold, genuinely hungry, sits at the communal supper and mumbles to his neighbours. A charity group is putting on a 'vegan feast' on Midsummer Common. He sits at a trestle table and eats the delectables. He is conscious of smelling slightly pissy. He hasn't washed for weeks. But people press against him like he's living, and warm, and worth being close to. Someone nearby—already fed—is sitting on the grass playing a guitar and singing about the table and eating and the town of Cambridge. They are celebrating nature and its bounty. Harold is thinking of Monsanto eating the town, of atomic waste strewn here and there, of the military getting its hooks in, of gender imbalance and barely suppressed racism wanting to burst out. He is really thinking those things as he tucks into delicious food. He even thinks the word 'delicious' which he hasn't conceptualised in decades. He is trying to hear and understand the lyrics. Pure celebration. He reasons the performer is stoned. But then he forgets, and is wondering what Trent Reznor would do with Mahler's Third, which is now working through its six notions of address and reception in his itchy head—maybe he has lice?

*

Each movement of my making sense has left me more removed from my beginnings. I originate then disperse. A friend, and he was from a Jewish family in an isolated town in Western Australia where Catholics went to one school and the rest went to another, other than the kids of some wealthy Anglicans who boarded their kids down in the city with an eye on executive positions in the mining industry, the arms industry or even a seat in parliament . . . A friend. My friend. In the state school there was I and the bullies who aligned themselves with murderous groups and tortured and raped and got away with it. Every cell of my genitals and sensitive areas of the body was poked and prodded, exposed and laughed over. By boys and girls. But only now I look back and understand as WWII history was taught to us and the library copy of *Mein Kampf* got so thumbed that my friend whom I loved and wanted to emulate had to turn against me and join the pack and become a BIG MAN and tell my secrets in order to disract and hide from the grotesque antisemitism he experienced. Rise and fall? No, it doesn't have to work that way. I live at a tangent to the mildew, my lungs shot and the sanatorium wanting me, it's true, but I can't feel its love. Alone. What pain he must have had. His difference he rightly cherished always under siege. To stand out but also 'fit in'—to join the rage against the 'Middle East' because OPEC and the oil crisis had parents up in arms their gas guzzlers angry at being starved of oil and choked without 'gas'. All of that was a way out and there were no students who openly avowed 'the Middle East' back then so he turned to the lukewarm Christians and even the fundamentalist Christians and said we have a common enemy and you feel torn, but remain loyal to his memory his agony because he had the most massive conscience of anyone you've ever known and his crimes against the sanctity of the body of others were committed to gain cred with bullies. But still he did these things and still he said these things against the grain with all laws breaking up and the grain flying with the chaff against origins. Such capacity for love and harm. The hurt a colonial world expects one to dish out to others if you're to be allowed in—allowed in and to stay on stolen land. The soaring music the soaring biography the slip of mood to see the masterpiece completed, *What sin what mystery what unpleasantries on a night of triumph, a night of celebration*—one of the big ones of European culture, of music! I wonder what he is doing. We are the same living age. We hear the cymbals, are relieved by the strings and woodwind, by the brass tacks of survival. He has a family, he has stayed with his origins. I am nowhere, especially not here. Tonight you can sleep on the floor—your heavy breathing that verges on snoring (do I embarrass you?) gives me relief. It is selfish of me I know, I know, I know. Always the way, always the flourish, always the self-righteous platitude. The baton signs off—its signature at the apogee of someone else's achievement. Or the collective endgame?

Symphony No. 4

CALLED A STALKER when shuffling makes you seem too present? Into a consciousness. Balloons. Crayons. Cuisenaire rods. Height marked on the door frame. Boob Tube Game Party Fun for Ages 6 to 60. Boob Tube Race. Milton Bradley ownership of sensibility, imagination. Commercial sites of recall. But had to win because it wasn't a contact sport, not really. Little places one shines in. Down down marble down, section by section, escape hatch port of entry. Model for Sky Lab? Crawl through from Apollo Capsule to Lunar Module. NASA private contracts. 3D printer space junk vaporise launch pad and biosphere. Shit to burn up eventually, maybe. Our low degrading orbits, higher orbit ambitions. Geostationary Boob Tubes.

*

Demimonde is a small club and not at all cool where Harold came from.

*

My ghost life is one of watching and hearing and feeling other ghost lives. They fill me. They are enough. I don't need other contact. Their non-contact is bliss and terror.

Back spasms are a sign they're entering. Around the region of the kidneys. Once, climbing to the top of Victoria Peak, a bird of prey ghosting me, I collapsed to the path in spasms. I thought a mosquito had found a way into my soul—an exchange of my blood for something it had picked up on its tour of veins. But in a small room above a shop a fortune teller would let me know: double ghosts entered you at once. From behind. She offered stimulating herbs which I refused.

The connection with malfeasance is often erroneous, though not always.

Those damned sleigh bells. Snowqueenphobia. Traumatised me hearing them as a kid coming with polar bears in the garden outside the kitchen window in the summer darkness, the heat making the Shelltox fly strips sweat in their cages.

Don't be such a bitter child. You have all your life before you. Joy! But I did like my own space, researching why it was all empirical. Why the rocks, why seeds found dirt in granite crevices and grew, traversed by wolf spiders. Why.

Why knees hurt most praying on thin cushions in church, on the concrete floor, on the floorboards, depending where. Suburbs or country town. Or family chapels on the edge of the clearing. The D9 irritating the gravel, then disembowelling the earth. The high-viz prophets sounding out the next spot to dig a sample pit. To find.

It wasn't your book, it was a girl cousin's book. But she let you read it, read it all. And the 'feminine' got inside and haunted and opened the whirlpool of creativity, a secret permission to write facts and fiction as one and the same, material spirit and consequence, decodings of the brutal. Meeting the women pigshooters confused you, but then you understood that, you were sure, too. On the side of the pigs, but understanding the variations on a theme.

You spend too much time thinking over your childhood.

Maybe. But it's not a case of critiquing my lot. Bothering over how much I got. Whether I was treated perfectly or imperfectly. Whether my parents or a parent were as I wanted them to be, relations and sibling, a lack of friends, a belief that I could see wrongs being done by adults, the world. But it was about seeing others wanting to extend their power over me and others, to have more than their share. Yes, I did measure biscuits, and I did like accumulating money and making a good deal, but then one day that too went bust and I detested money and realised it was a substitute for the power I didn't have in the change room or on the sporting field or competing for the affections of other kids. I was maybe not likeable because I was odd—alone in myself, reading girl's books and boy's book and 'doing science' and experimenting and trying to prove the existence of God. Maybe.

But can't you see how self-indulgent this is?

We are the children we were.

Another platitude.

I don't want this conversation. You shouldn't harass the women and the girl.

We have a lot in common. I lost my child—a girl of the same age—two years ago.

I am sorry . . .

Services handed her over to her father.

Why?

It's rude to ask, but I will tell you. Because her father complained that I am an unfit mother. Because he is rich.

What does 'unfit mother' mean?

Nothing. I am not a mother and he is not a father. They are bullshit roles applied by the state. No, to tell the truth, I don't have a daughter. I've never had children.

I don't like the State. I never know what the truth is anyway.

See, we have things in common, too.

*

The white-faced heron was facing south again this morning. This afternoon it will be facing north. Not true north and maybe a few degrees off due south. Not spot-on cardinal points. This the sun from the east in the morning waking, and the shutdown sunset modulate the access to seeing below, parallax error. Refraction. Reflection. The water's modulation of content, of what's plucked out. And so I steered my way through the bullies, relying on the camouflage of change, of patterns, of repetition, of sudden deviation/s. I reversed the earth, and the sun temporarily rose in the west.

*

Happiest moments? You ask me while I am listening to NIN's *The Downward Spiral*? An album with consequences?

No, while we're listening to Mahler's 4th.

Yes, the wires cross in my head. A long drag across a violin string can drag me into a Reznor moment. Into the shit around his being.

Happiest moments in childhood?

Hearing through a relative that the night parrot wasn't extinct. I thought of the night parrot as a single bird, and it was surviving. Then I read that night PARROTS were extinct. Now we know they're not. But I was happy THE night parrot was out there, on the edge of salt lakes, flying fast and low and making its special sound. I tried to ghost myself at night and fly inland, far inland, and find it to say hello, to converse and learn and get back to my body by morning when I had to go to school and confront my sexual assaulters—the boys who pulled my penis, the girls who poled me. Facts. Ghosting is a fact. Is this a confession?

Is it?

Happiness. That Reznor album was linked to Columbine. I have seen guns, many guns, and heard kids and adults express desires to use them on animals, and people. Massacres can happen wherever there are the weapons to facilitate them. So many people harbour hatreds mixed with anger and fear and guns take them over the edge. They are so easy to use and the adrenaline boost carries the day. It's a build-up and release. I've heard it said. When I handled guns as a kid my only fear was that I would use them to hurt animals, and especially birds, and I did. I hated myself. I never wanted to hurt people with guns. But then, I never wanted to hurt animals. And birds were vectors out of my body—they were the wings to my ghost self. But then, I thought about shooting myself which means I could shoot a person, even if that person was myself. So I rejected guns, and I rejected the lies around guns. The rejection was when the happiness came. The guns were unhappiness. They were immanence and latent horror. They are the lies of skill and accuracy. They are penetration fantasy devices that silence the victims at the moment of entry. My grandfather was shot in the head. Before that, he fired weapons. He shot guns in two wars. He was a shooter condoned by the army, by the state, by the act of war. What happens on the battlefield never stays on the battlefield. He melted his medals down. He did not cast them into ammunition and fire them back at the oppressors, the army, the state. But said they were the calm before the storm. Unholy relics. Captain Scarlet serving the enemy.

*

Happiness?

Yes, just pure joy without a care in the world.

Happiness. Sort of word they deploy for big events in minimalist packages. Supposed to be enough in itself: works ironically, literally, however you want or don't want.

It remains a question.

Yes, it does. But it's not for me. It's just a word. And I don't trust words. Your dragging them out of me. I've talked more to you than I've talked to anyone for years. And years.

Happiness.

A statement.

Yes. And the river finding its way through the subsoil into your basement.

They drain the Cam every year and clear out the bicycles that have been dumped. And the ducks hang around bemused on the banks.

Happiness!

Emphatic. Yes. Happiness. I remember. I remember having a friend who wanted to make a nuclear bomb. He thought I could help him. Instead of saying I didn't know how, I said: Sorry, I won't help you in your crime against humanity, against the planet. I believed I could do anything if I put my mind to it. And if I put my mind to it, I wasn't willing to translate into a material reality. I said, I won't do it! I was happy! with my decision.

Mass noun. The state of being . . . happy.

Yes. I was most happy when. When I. When I remember a day—with its good and bad—from my childhood that I had completely forgotten. When it comes back to me. I would like to remember every moment of my existence, in detail. To spend my time replaying it.

In your basement room?

Or loft. Or the cave I once lived in by the sea. Anywhere, really. Here and now.

Can you bring a day back you think you'd lost right now—retrieve something you can't remember retrieving since you became conscious of a desire to retrieve?

Let me think . . .

It is a conscious process of retrieval.

Sometimes. Sometimes not. Here, now . . . something.

I tell you . . . No prompts to memory, nobody to recount something that acts as a trigger . . . remember that day when you, when we . . . or a photo taken by someone else you've not seen before and there you are. None of that. I have nothing—no memorabilia of me. Just you and your coffee and me and my green tea—thanks for the tea, by the way.

That's fine, says the sab woman. Now, you were saying?

I tell you, I am remembering a school day and I am eight, not an age I remember a lot from. Not usually. But I am eight and maybe four months. It is mid-year and cold. The days are short. I am at my desk in front of the teacher's desk, at my desk alongside a boy with blonde almost white hair. He is scratching inside his ear with his pencil. The pencil is blunt and the teacher has told him to sharpen it over the bin. But he's not hearing—he has a pencil in one ear and is hard of hearing in the other. That is why he has been seated close to the front of the class. As close as you can get, though maybe I am seated closer because when the teacher gets up to teach at the blackboard I am closer. I remember it is not long after school has started and though the sun is up and shining through the window and it is a clear cold day and the day is short I am full of the possibilities of the day. I am disturbed by the pencil in the ear scratching the skin around the earhole and lean away because I don't want to accidentally bump the boy whose name I can't remember though it will come to me. I don't want to bump the pencil and drive it through his hearing gear into his brain. I know there's an ear and eardrum and inner ear and a brain in close proximity, I know that and I know about pencils. His name was Vincent. I liked Vincent though we weren't friends. He never told me what he thought of me but didn't bother me much—just petty annoyances—and I always spoke up but never in his good ear which was now blocked and obscured by a 2B pencil. First the wooden end with chewed paint and wood and then the blunt lead end. I said to him, Be careful Vincent you don't hurt your brain. And he smiled, and removed the pencil, and said, I have to sharpen it over the bin.

*

The deep-ripping of subsoil hurt my soul.

*

A family concert. I played triangle. There were three pianos in a country hall hired for the occasion. My grandfather, my mother, my auntie, all playing at once. We were singing along. I was playing the triangle. Cousins—some distant—were playing clarinets, violins, and a bugle. There was a solo performance of electric guitar—a rendition of Hendrix's take of the Star Spangled Banner. A take of a take. A shredding. There were friends of family inside the hall. I had no friends, but I could have had friends. I chose not to have friends. I didn't want anyone to hear me playing the triangle, though I kept time and never overplayed. I came and went at the right time. Three pianos speaking—and arguing—with each other. From Scarborough Fair to Bach organ pieces transposed for piano. There was a buffet—all the family and friends brought dishes. I drank a red fizzy drink I was usually forbidden. This was twenty years before 'Music for 3 Pianos' by Harold Budd, R. Garcia and D. Lentz. [I am hearing 'La Muchacha De Los Sueños Dorados'! as I speak.] And so much of it was overplaying of different tunes but picking up near the ends so there were short overlays followed by long runs solo sounding like conventional renditions of compositions for single pianos. It was, I hate to say, magical. I recognised my selfishness in wanting the occasion entirely to myself especially when there were ninety people in that hall and it was sweaty and people were overwrought and among them were some who hated others and would rather be out pig shooting. But it brought people together and there was singing and the Anglican minister clapped his hands and roused the quiet ones to action. All this *soft pedalling* backwards. And those three upright pianos—the one my grandfather played was slightly out of tune but he worked with that and said he felt comfortable being the one out of tune, his daughters playing newer in-tune pianos that hadn't even been jolted slightly out of tune by their transport from respective country houses, the old piano played by grandfather Harold being the town hall upright smashed and cajoled by every music-hating kid in town. Not that I ever believed any of the kids hated music. That was just a show. A necessary display of contempt. I struck my triangle and shrank away though took it seriously. In that paradox I was lost.

*

The stalker declares: You don't cope well with being shamed.

No, no I don't. It used to anger me, now it makes me want to crawl away.

Is it shame that has brought you here, to Cambridge?

I feel tempted to perform the old 'switch-a-roo' on you and asked what so disturbed you in your childhood that you stalk people.

You are benefiting from the social energy of my 'stalking' at the moment. I am supplying you with green tea in a 'pleasant' café.

I don't like scare quotes painted in the air, thank you.

Well, there you go!

Goes what?

Nothing. You asked about my childhood? Australian like yours but a more recent generation. I am what some would call the end of Generation X. If you believe in such garbage.

A marketing tool. Nothing more.

Agreed. My childhood was Australian but not Western Australian as such, though we did live in a seaside suburb of Perth for two years when I was ten to twelve. It's called Safety Bay, do you know it?

Of course I do.

Well, my old man worked at the nickel refinery at Kwinana. And my mother worked in a local supermarket part-time. And I got into trouble and went to children's court on a fairly regular basis. Actually, my childhood wherever we were living was one of crime.

You were an arsonist, I am guessing.

Sometimes, but mostly a thief and a 'peeping Tom', as they call them. Well, not really a female Peeping Tom . . . I just liked to watch happy families being happy while watching television in their living rooms.

An apprenticeship.

Yes. I worked hard at it, Harold. Can I call you Harold? I have already but you look uncomfortable when I say your name.

I am not a fan of names. Of identities. I don't believe I have one.

No identity?

No.

I like that a lot.

You like it only because of subterfuge. I am not interested in subterfuge, of working from shadows to exploit. I don't wish to take advantage.

We all take advantage one way or another.

That's just too easy. I have no respect for crime, Harold insists.

I also liked to swim as a child. I swam in Safety Bay. I didn't swim any particular stroke—really, what I did was an amalgamation of them all. I liked swimming on Kwinana Beach most of all—with the factories looming and the fall-out. I thrived on it, then they took me away. We went to Weipa after that. The Gulf. Bauxite. It was Camalco back then. I swam there, too. At great risk. Don't swim, fish, they said. You'll live longer. Red Beach—I plotted my escape. I stole a four-wheel drive when I was fourteen and drove all the way to Cairns. There were half a dozen jerry cans of fuel strapped to the roof. In Cairns I found a dope dealer—I was good at that—and sold the vehicle. I told them all wild croc stories but mostly I talked about the serene waters of Safety Bay.

The Camalco Act—1957. Aboriginal reserve status revoked. The red cliffs of prosperity. And now, I read, the Australian government wants to be a top-ten arms exporter. Western Australia's left-lite government with its ex-military Premier is in there, boots and all.

You keep up with things, don't you Harold!

I look at the internet in the Cambridge Town library every now and again.

I have seen you in there.

You have? I guess you have. Why do you harass the woman and her daughter? It is wrong and I want you to stop it.

The Marlowe Dramatic Society formed in Cambridge in the early part of the twentieth-century with an aim to further the works of Marlowe and Shakespeare. Marlowe was a spy. That's why. And by the by, why do you hang out with that hideous animal libber woman—the fox obsessive?

I find it difficult to talk with more than one person at once. Many voices coming in and out of focus distract me. I become self-conscious and feel even more alone. But talking like this—one on one—makes me feel threatened. You are an awful person.

You have lost your confidence, Harold.

Yes. But that's not a bad thing. That's the point. Spy. Yes, you are a spy. I do not wish Marlowe's fate on you. I detest violence.

Though you were involved in plenty of it when you were younger—and instigated a fair bit of it, I am sure.

How can you know that? What do you know? To whom have you been speaking? At what keyholes have you been listening? I mutter in my sleep, I know that. The sab woman has betrayed me?! That's why you make sarcastic remarks about her — to distract me. She has been listening and repeating, hasn't she? Don't try and keep a straight face with me. With me—I sound absurd to myself. This is not what I want, these self-reflexive obsessional thoughts, these accruing paranoias. I want none of it and none of you. I am alone. Standing outside, watching it happen. He's shy, they'd say when I was a small child, watching their strangeness. And then I'd turn away and they would say, He's developing a social problem—he needs to be seen to. Who were those people. Teachers? The Bin Teacher. Parents of other children watching you getting your case sorted as you left school. Walking behind you with their children, who are laughing. You leave the path and stand in front of a lamppost, stand, looking up, away from them. He does that in class, the children say, as you look up into the wires. But the you—I—is wondering why the magpies don't get electrocuted because you—the I—have seen electrocuted magpies. Or is it the person on the checkout till, saying to mother, Why doesn't he look at people—he hides his face. Shy. Shy till he dies. The bell of the till chiming, the bells of the church of commerce. That's what it was, and though without the words then, I knew. Always have. Sacrificed at the altar of capitalism, though not by my mother, never. She said the triangle is percussion and the backbone of the full orchestra—never let the first violinist tell you otherwise, Harry. She too, sometimes . . . rarely, called me Harry. It was the sab woman, wasn't it? Sleeping in the vicinity. I let her into proximity. Sleeping is exposure. She says I am asexual. She says of herself that she's, *Very* sexual. She thinks of herself as a fox. She says she doesn't like or get off on sexual violence. She does not want to be a violated fox. But she likes to rut. She says I could be sexual, too, if I allowed myself. It doesn't repulse me. I just don't see the point. I am just not interested. It. It. It is irrelevant. As innuendo was at school. As the filthy jokes and limericks I had forced on me that lodged never to leave because poetry in all its forms does that to me—goes in and sticks. I cannot unremember, cannot destroy it. Sticks like a toxin. Adheres. Those filthy misogynist jokes I had thumped into me. I said them once at a gathering to show how sick we all are, and I was excommunicated as some kind of sick demon. I tried to explain this is the truth behind the 'tolerance', the new equality, the lip-service, the lies of freedom. It lurks, implanted in Baby Boomers and fed to generation X and chipped-in in the Y's. Lurking ready to oppress when the apocalypse does its tricks. It was the sab woman and that saddens me. For in her there is actually hope. She does something. She stops the aristocrats and their hangers-on. She detests the cruelty. And yet, it is cruel of her to tell you, you of all people. People. You who betray me and stalk her friend. You who are a danger. You who are the messenger. The dragon. The winged beast. Apocalypse.

Yes, it's the sab woman. All you say is true. She *has* betrayed you, Harold.

It doesn't help to hear that. You smile? That's just too easy. Listen, listen . . . hear . . . they're piping Johnny Cash's version of 'Hurt'. Is it Radio One? Do they care?

No, it's not. It doesn't even sound like it. You have

auditory ossification. Or 'thought process in reverberation'. You are hearing inside your own head.

You are as dated as I am. We are both doomed in reverb. I knew a man who believed Christendom was Christendoom. True.

It was the sab woman. It is good to blame. Isn't it. Isn't it!

*

You are only hanging around with those foreigner kids because you are so weird, Harold. Harold mused over the word 'weird'—weirding. Weirding way. Wyrding way. Wyrd. I am weird, they say, You weirdo, get away from us. You smell. Of urine. But I wee in a toilet and don't have wee on me. I am clean. No, you stink. Weirdo. It's a funny word that makes laughs and disgust. Foreign kids—the school is mainly English migrant and British heritage second or third generation. Foreign is the Japanese Kids, the Burmese kid, the Malaysian kid, the three Aboriginal kids. And some others that look *dubious*. Untalking together. But nothing chummy, not like *They're a Weird Mob* which is an Irishman being Italian for the sake of demonstration—Mum has that on her bookshelf. Our shelves. I can take it off the shelf and read. Grundy. Undie. Undie eater. Not fun like the weird mob. Different weird. The weird mob hate the weird, or the weird are the weirdos or the weirdos hate the weird. All chummy in their hate, kids arrowing in. I *was*—I remain in the reunions they have in which I am the deletion, the ignored at best moment on class photos, still a laugh connected to the public glory of my ex and her little jokes about my failings in the glossies then the websites then the social media and now a hashtag for something I was I don't recognise, a past. All of that is me, now, my lungs affected by mildew from the river seeping horizontal but bikes being ridden the wrong way and hitting me on the hip the shoulder, Hey! You're not supposed to ride that way. Every day dozens of bikes stolen in Cambridge and taken north and south and west, far west to be sold and locked up outside pubs. I stand and listen to the penny whistle, dog at the player's feet, player against the pissy wall of a stationary store, a chain store, a place of livelihoods and invoices. The shrill is a weirding truth, is the recorder blare of the defiant. I liked the haters at school but they didn't like me. I didn't like their hate, but I knew the frustration. I was just frustrated with different things. Flutes lie, I said to the teacher, who whacked me across the knuckles with a recorder. You are not going to be a soloist in my class, he or she said. He or she? Whacked across the knuckles for refusing to understand pronouns. S/he's a weirdo, neuter you and nothing to do with we, who cluster and encircle you weirdos—four corners, out of the jungle, jungle bunnies. my father says we fought to keep the likes of you out. But I was already in and my grandfather fought in two wars and said that we are invaders making war on people who have been here tens of thousands of years and he didn't like war and he says imperialists wanted to kill everyone who wasn't possessable and then lost most of it because they exhausted themselves but then looked for ways to get it all back. You're a weirdo and not even a real boy and you can't play with the girls so you're alone with that foreign muck and you eat food that makes you stink and you wee yourself and though your skin looks white it's actually quite dark and you've snuck in from somewhere my father who runs a real estate business says people like you have infiltrated and we have to watch out who we sell properties to. All those decades ago? Liberty? I am you. Me, too. Toughen up, mate, someone says . . . It's not all sweetness and light.

*

Hear a voice—a celestial voice. It is a woman singing, but why couldn't it be a man? Not a girl singing? Not a boy? A person is singing. That's true. Climb the tallest tree in the back garden, the one with the golden crown so far up it can be seen from school, even from boats on the river. It is not a really old tree, just one that has grown phenomenally fast. An aspiring tree, an aspirational tree, a tree that provokes and evokes comments. A language tree. What type of tree? It is unfamiliar. Exotic. From one of the Capes or via one of the Capes? A seed planted in strange sand not really soil just black sand that drains well and paydirt, off & aspiring. A massive triangle of a tree. Climb it and search out that voice across suburbs and outskirts, up and down river, in the circulatory system of plain then Scarp and through the depleted forests into the wheat regions. The voice that speaks to the child but is not a pied piper is not laying a false trail luring to doom. No siren perversion you need worry about ahead of time but there's no real second-guessing, is there? What will decide a behavioural pattern a set of sexual responses as puberty kicks in and expectation cowers the body into corners to burst out in shame? A shiver, a soothing balm, all at once. Sanctuary, the sway up there the inevitability of snap or topple the view at a cost the falling down the rising up the inverted pendulum of curiosity and need. The voice. A range not even describable, especially given the constraints on input even with Sunday School singing, even with nudges towards the choir though the voice doesn't quite work. Hypotenuse. You see, idiophone, it's the non-closure, the gap, the suggestion of all sides meeting, the pitch wandering where the crevice will take it. Such affirmations such reclamations such a roll of the southerly to take the tip of the tall fast-growing tree down towards the ground but interrupted by fence or shed or other impediment, the searching earth the vegetal fork of lightning the reverberation. Timpani, glockespiel, sleigh bells, tam-tam, cymbals, triangle . . . listen, listen 'Das himmlische Leben' . . .

In search of a new instrument, deciding to go back to what he'd lost, Harold came across this at the Cambridge Town Library:

ALAN ABEL 6" WAGNER/MAHLER TRIANGLE

OVERVIEW

— Crisp Clean Attack
— Emphasis on Dark Overtones
— Darker, Germanic Sound- Great for Wagner, Mahler, Strauss, Etc.

— 6" Length

ITEM DETAILS

—This 6" Wagner/Mahler Triangle was created by Alan Abel (former Associate Principal Percussionist of the Philadelphia Orchestra) and is designed to provide a heavier, darker sound appropriate for the works of Mahler, Wagner, and other Germanic composers.

The AA3 produces crisp, clean attacks that Abel Triangle owners expect with a particular emphasis on lower overtones to create a dark, warm sound that just sounds right for moody, epic Germanic symphonic works (and anything else in the same emotional area).[1]

But he had no money. He returned to the Mahler biography, listening out for the lost voice. The voice from the tip of the tree that aspired, that bent, that grew too fast. In his heart, a harp was dominating, and this lulled and bothered him. Pluck pluck went the night parrot walking the banks of the Cam. The colonial repercussions slew him. He wondered about the funeral boat in the decrepit boathouse. He wondered about his narrative collusion. He knew he was being stalked but felt he was being useful in keeping the harasser away from the woman and her daughter. Feeling

[1] http://www.lonestarpercussion.com/Concert/Triangles/Alan-Abel-AA3.html

useful, he tuned his ear into the tune that distributed itself through the biosphere like the pollution from one of Elon Musk's heavy life rockets—eddying about locally, before finding a way through the drives and barrier of currents, to disperse, to speak 'you to you' in the Jerry Lewis reality he was turning to. He, Harold. That is.[2]

Harold remembers seeing and hearing the 4th at the Perth Concert Hall on two occasions. On the second occasion, he was seated up in the lower gallery next to Lucida and it was the second movement and she was whispering in his ear, Don't you love that wandering violin, I love tunings that don't comply. It is death, whispered Harold back, annoyed that she spoke. Yes, but so much life in this, what child wouldn't want heaven. My music machine works for all people no matter what age: through it they can see the heavens as nature, which is what it is. A baby has access to the music machine if they want it. And Lucida suppressed a laugh, because she loved Harold so, but she said, Harold, your music machine is only in your head and no one else can access it!

Harold loved the heavenly song. He loved the way the symphony finished with sympathy. As he lifted with the blooming voice of the soprano, he thought, Mahler would have loved her, which might or might not have been good for the soprano. Soon, soon, he would sing to Alma. But not yet. Who was singing? Was Harold singing to Mahler, to Alma, to the soprano, to Lucida and the precarity of their love? The orchestra melded and convulsed and blended

---

[2] Is This An Unreliable Footnote to the 4th and the Music Machine?

and flowered: he followed the trail of lifted horns and sawing bows, he rolled with the kettle drums, and the sleigh bell recharged his irony of unbelonging. He wondered how he would have heard this music had he been born at Windermere or Grasmere, the vision of fallout creeping over the mountains, settling. He wondered about the walk to the opera house in Vienna. My machine would have been tuned differently, had the case itself been different.

I will have to give up the music machine, thought Harold, as he travelled roads of his childhood and realised that bulldozers with tree-pushers would have uprooted the great marri and jarrah trees of the range, that orchards would grow over the bonfire heaps and the poison sprays would make the 'hills mist'. A voting trend. His child's heaven devastated, as the scrub rolled back interior was another step of his childhood . . . heaven.

I am the confusion of two violins—one in the hand of the concertmaster, and before them. I am the soprano who will wait until the time comes for them to stand and enounce. I am the triangle, always the triangle.

I am confused by the giant bonfires of jarrah trees that a short while before had been housing red-tailed black cockatoos decapping the fruits, the honkey nuts plopping to the ground like a single strike by a mallet on the middle C of a xylophone. I am confused because Mahler and songs and instruments are in my head and I can't see the wood for the trees or the flames. Should I have responded then, knowing the pain but protest unformed. In the country with family, in the hall listening to pianos—more than one, unusual in the hall. That's up from the hills, up through the jarrah and marri all the way through the wandoo to the York gum and jam tree. Machinery of the orchestra, prepared piano of 1942—grandfather at war, deploying 'primitive', the jungle fears, the irony of language-lack, of the cage the John Cage he was half aware through the aether was transcribing and transmitting to the Great Equaliser, Rabaul. The Salt flush of education and the mates protectorship of doomsday machine before its time. Jungle division camouflage unit. Primitive, that's what we were, said Harold's grandfather. O six volcanoes O campnosperma O ficus O large-eared sheath-tailed bat! O consequence O policy from capitals and bunkers O people whose land serves as a fighting platform. O death in heaven. I was a child when I heard it all I was a child in the bush a child visiting the city a child compiling strands of family and lost in musical gatherings a child with a case standing pigeon-toed in a line that ejected me and a rubbish-bin kid and a piss-tray kid and a dizzy with *Let's Join In It's Going to Begin Songs To Sing* through the grey PA the grey soundeye over the blackboard so who can own that imposition who can suck life dry through an old kookaburra through a gum tree as I—we—were inoculated with BELONGING. But my grandfather had one eye and was one-eyed and over 40 or was 40 fighting at Tobruk? A one-eyed old man in New Britain? How did that come to be? I was a child listening, listening, and inventing my music machine. He told me the species of plants and animals in the jungle. The birdcalls. The 'chatter of the Jap 99 Light Machine Gun'. I learnt my capital letters this way. And then he said, of the Germans and the Japanese soldiers, They probably didn't want to be there any more than us . . . He said that for humanity, whether it was true or not. In retrospect, he said. What's retrospect? I asked. Harold, it is the truth. It was 1941, and for 241 days we . . . and the locals were written out of the pain, the anguish. We were looking to defy Hell and rewrite Heaven—install a version that might last.

Harold shook and whistled and clapped his hands like a child possessed.

To keep the heaven going to keep his child self-seeing the wonder the glory as death closed in and took away the oxygen provided by trees took away the trees as the heaven of artificial lighting of entertainment took hold of the night he couldn't let go of Mahler's vision of a child's vision of heaven he needed it to sustain to process the little betrayals of human by humans of nature by humans of ideals by human with each shuffling walk through town—the bit of rubbish dropped into the Cam, the indifference to a begging cup, the smirk of one business partner thinking of how a degree of advantage had been gained over the other without the sun shining brightly on the reality.

I was a child when I first heard the 4th. Four times I have heard the 4th 'live'. I was the only child in an audience of maybe one thousand. I was uncomfortable in the hard seat, and I had to lean on my mother to see the orchestra—all of the orchestra. It wasn't as big an orchestra as Mahler conjured, but it was big enough and I wanted to see all the players at the same time, my eyes flashing from cellos to harp, from percussion to violins, from *from* from. The conductor told a truth I understood but resisted—in my head, it was being conducted without the smoothness, without the flow. It was jagged and heaven was frightening. I was never lulled in the last two movements, I never drifted off on my mother's lap. I itched and twisted and rebelled, and thought this is an adult's heaven not a kid's heaven but I knew all adults thought kids made better heavens in their heads, in their bedrooms, in the garden, out in the bare aching paddocks where ghosts moved around the trees that once were. Death's violin is the adult playing, but so is the rest. But in the 'out of tune' I could follow the line to my future, to living in the shadows, to being lost in the expat lies of creativity, of getting away from unbelonging. To unbelong in the hoodwink of sleighbells, of strings in harmony.

In the back of the station-wagon, breaking the top of Greenmount Hill, past the Leap where the warriors chased the colonists—a half story half formed, but one that never seemed to add up, Chipper's Leap, that was it, where the plaque on the granite was overwritten erased rewritten. Now I call a dialectic now I am overwhelmed with sadness, with events leading to events. With consequences. With the litany of deaths (the colonial killing fields) that lead to such an encounter. To another death. Cause and effect and sadness. I spiral into myself because I have nowhere to go, which is nothing in the face of. A hundred years after the 'event' (1932) they—they, the colonial residuals (the enforcers) placed this plaque: *On the 3rd of February 1832. John Chipper and*

Reuben Beacham a boy of fourteen, while driving a cart from Guildford to York, were attacked by natives near this spot. Beacham was killed but Chipper although speared, escaped and leaped from this rock, now known as Chipper's Leap, and eventually reached Governor Stirling's house at Woodbridge. I could recall completely if needs be, I could, climbing out of the city out of Midland off the plain, the Swan coastal plain that would (has the time of such prophecy passed or just shifted tense?) go under the sea when the Big Wave came, and I felt relief and agony at once, for all those down there who would be swept away and closer to the stars the canopy of jarrah the nightbirds and roosting cockatoos under with stars flashing through looking out the side windows with sleep, Harold, sleep *sleep* from Mum in the front, driving out to where grandfathers dwell uneasily in their war memories where relatives take us in where the city is where I will go and where I will come from in the confusion or interlacing of place that stars the representatives of heaven and fire and solar systems and telescope eyes bringing the Empyrean into the wagon lying under blankets on a folding mattress, thin so the car speaks through the tyres the wheels the axles the chassis the board under which the spare tyre is kept and I fear a blowout and Mum on the side of the road jacking the car in blackness other than the heaven of stars. And though in my ears in my head the low hum of the 4th, it moves away as I lull into sleep into displacement into the livingness of unawakedness and I remember knowing that the 4th is an adult's waking version of heaven as they fret after their lost childhoods and that it is nothing to do with me and what surrounds in the national park and beyond.

The residues of welcome and throwing goodwill to the machines, to the machines that would come to upturn the ground horse-drawn then self- propelled overturning inside outing. I dream of Sunshine Harvesters eating me and wake suddenly, repelled by the ubiquity of station-wagon sleeping and wondering why my mother is so far away. She is listening to a cassette tape of the 4th, I have woken in the second movement, inside the violin. I can't keep pace with anything. And then the world falls another degree out of focus, another tone above the continuum. I am a sci-fi kid. There's a silence, a blank, then a, Hello hello hello . . . then silence blank with just the compulsion of the six-cylinder holder engine, the tyres slightly distressed on the rough bitumen. And then the 4th drops back in on as 'Das himmlische Leben' attempts to reset the world in its own image. What? says his Mum, What on earth? messing with the cassette player's controls. I shock out of my skin, I hover above myself, moving as the car moves.

And driven out of confusion and half-awakedness and the stars piercing him through the windows, and guilt, that horrendous guilt of past present future that will dominate his narrative, his loves and their failures, he bursts out, Sorry, Mum, I put tape over the 'record holes' to see if it could still be recorded over—it was an experiment, Sorry sorry sorry! You've erased Mahler! said his mother, with an irritation that upset him, but an irritation that softened into a strange laughter that spooked him more than anything else in his life to that point. A castigating affection.

Later, later, I was told to run a magnet over the tape to rewrite memory. It would empty and you could refill. That's the technology, that's how they make new stories? I wondered if a trace would remain, a fragment of a note. A fragment of original intent. That's how I reconfigure it now, making where I sleep or try to sleep a home. If you object to the word 'home', rest—*rest*—assured, I do, too, but only in the context of myself, not with regard to you. What happens when your limbs become silver birches and your scalp fly agaric? I must work with others, I must reconnect—I must smile when they grimace at me, I must try to lift from my stop and walk upright. I feel I should douse myself in something sweet-smelling, make myself more welcoming, be more welcoming to the others. I will stare through a window in Lion's Yard and look like I would consume if I had the cash, the disposable income. But that might make them fear me more. I will move on. On and on. I do not have an iphone. I do not have gel technology in my shoes. I do not know who won the football last night. And to keep Mahler in my head I must keep listening to the records, keep the grooves spiralling towards their centres. Cosmology.

Symphony No. 5

I have loved, I know it now, said Harold. I could love again, and know it. Be aware as I am loving. No mistaking the beginnings in death though. Love fertilised by grief. Forced into the march of care, our vulnerability and reliance on others caring for us. The slightest lapse can make it tough. But good enough is good enough. Love learns fast—eager and hungry, never satisfied. No. So often more indifferent than advertised. Births deaths marriages birth deaths marriages births deaths marriages birth deaths marriages births deaths marriages birth deaths marriages births deaths marriages birth deaths marriages births deaths marriages birth deaths marriages births deaths marriages birth deaths marriages.

What do you do you do with it when you don't have the hooks of the Big Religions—or the big denominations of religions—to hang it all on. Catholicism gives you the codes for love, Anglicanism gives you a breakaway code for love. Love filters down, branches, plays its tricks, resorts to the machine of the religion, the shadow of the state or a state in itself. Love has to accord. But what when not. It is not a question. Over. The particles. The articles. The prepositions. The pronouns.

Who is telling me love is worthless without integrity. It comes in versions, of course, and a profit (living, life, breathing and and and eating and shitting) comes from each and every one. Change marketed as positive. Love without plagiarism. Integrity of self-testing, running it through. Original per billions per space per accumulation of wealth. This equation we test on isolated spots. Islands? Love on islands.

You inkle.
We inkle.
I inkle.
They inkle. Harold inkles?
I gorged and purged. You see that. Didn't we?

*

I have loved in the dark places of the world. You cannot see or understand my love, but it has been there. The theatre people thought I was loveless, and made a thing about it, pointing out that my drug of choice was heroin not speed, which they said said it all. But my life was a ruin and in the darkness I wandered knowing my own wrongness and my colonial soul I wanted to shed. As I read *Heart of Darkness* I had shame for the experience that led to its writing, and shame for its writing, whilst relishing my insights into the darkness. But it wasn't the darkness exploited to show the universal darkness, the double entendre of entertainment, the making statements of human value and meeting a market demand. None of that. It was a horror of who I was and the love that glanced off white skin. I denied culture and dripped cultural accoutrements with my every denial of fashion, my refusal to go with the latest craze. In the narcotic haze I found dead peace, the peace of obliteration, the cliché of nothingness the Western subject hides behind to enjoy the drinks, the smokes, the movies, the books, the ponderings it likes while denying s/he/it is part of it. Fully part of it, and making it. It serves to have a dark white lord in the dark interior, as it serves to see a young Attenborough collecting and collating in new Guinea.

When I emerged from my cultural revolution, crossing my necessitated borders, fantasising an outside capitalism capitalist existence, I refused to acknowledge my appropriations. As if the rice fields—the paddies—were not where I walked, not where I saw the napalming of jungles in the Philippines as a confrontation with their movie death desiring, their blue-collar irritation to deer hunt the hippies. I was of all as great-great-grandmother was born in Boston before coming down down on the double-long journey and language redounded in the high seas where reactors fall to depths that will be plasticated so rapidly. All of that a prelude to the staggering movements towards parsing, the condensing of speech into packets to offset the unabsorbable reality of aloneness when the capacity for love has been so strong if innate.

I am pushed and shoved along Pitt Street, yearning north in search of the landbridge. Out out.

*

Alone, on the river's edge, you know you will love again one day. Fully and utterly. The river here, now, the Cam. A couple of old men are sitting on a wall drinking cider and smoking rollies. Though it looks like rain and is humid, they are happy watching the river flow by. Flow by. A river that can be drained. There are no punts on the river for no particular reasons. A thing of timing. But looking at them, Harold is thinking of old men on jetties on the Canning when he was a child—Gunbower Road, Springwood Avenue . . . sitting and drinking sherry, smoking rollies. Fucked up but sort of temporarily content. He'd speak with them sometimes, but it wasn't really a safe thing to do. One of them—once, and only one—flashed an off-shaped penis at him and laughed. That river that drew the rich mining executives who liked to watch the flow, the flow from the hills and beyond. Their wrecking places elsewhere. Harold could see a family of little grebes in his mind eye—a parent with a clutch of chicks, testing a brackish wetland pool. He could see a little egret manic in the shallows, spearing mosquito fish. The little birds. The little pied cormorant drying its wings. Sharp reeds with fruiting tops maces before the flag on mansion cross-ripple water paperbark twists some from the wealthy's buoys and pleasure craft and rose gardens daring water rats and gulls' thin white beaches clinging against lifestyle parks and dogpiss grass and trunks where an osprey on the promontory's last hurrah clings in the mess of codes. Mt Henry. Time in shadow of freeway where anarchy cried out and ate progress towards 'maturity', the graffiti that drove you to action and assessment and lithium. But love broods in the shallows, rivertide out and molluscs showing a path through to the channels. What is that you overhear as a bunch of people walk past? Was it: 'She showed us the spots, as they do.'? As they do? They? Do. The spots. The special zones, the locations, the points? Another voice, 'In Wellington there's a really good take-off point.' Take-off. A rip off a taking off? The spots. The points we repair to. The sites. This special investment of ourselves in *places*. To drag the analysis through puberty into a false maturity, to wonder if behind all the evil men shouting this and that around the riparian destruction and bush being cleared for freeway extensions and new highways and housing developments (they've gotta live somewhere!), if evil women also lurked? The machinery of maleness was so offensive you could see the semen clotting its works. It glued everything around it, forced it to do its will. You did not like or trust men. As a small child you'd put elastic bands around your penis to make it fall off like a ring around the lamb's tail on the farm. But it changed colour and hurt and the wee had to come out and it all went haywire. It sort of healed but the thinking stayed but not the abuse. It's a reaction to the expectation of love, you thought, you did, Harold, Harry, Hal. Your grandfather said groin injuries during the fighting in new Guinea brought screams from the projected darkness the white soldiers took in their packs everywhere, infection rapidly setting in. He said to Harold, I loved your grandmother before I met her. You were two when she died, as you know, as you know, as a narrative echo sounds out in the river where a boat was moored named after her by an earlier suitor. He died in the war. He, too, like so many of us. In the war. The WAR. The wars. He, too, in love with photos and letters. The technology of modern love. The flow. The flow. Bloodied rivers. Acid rain.

*

Those who destroy places, he said to himself, watching the magpie on the green. Those who destroy places, love. Also. They love also. Love, also. Also love. On the green—a cleared space grassed, watered. On the lawn. Those great lovers eye off the uncleared areas and want to make their estates. All the cleared and pillaged areas around and the aim for the bit of uncleared land they can obtain by influencing or stacking councils. Influencing public opinion. Making places for people to live, to enjoy the activities of living. A living. To be alive and live. To decease the marsupials whose DNA departs from their own 150 million years ago. Genome permission, which doesn't stick when the last guerrilla habitats are rolled back as well. But that's nowhere near, is it. Boom. Boom. Such job security in the rings of growth, old trees felled to make way. Magpie on the lawn, in colonial equivocation applied by makers of art, not by itself. Protection is 'red tape' so red tape is to be dispensed with. Dispenser. Tape off the dispenser. Grammar of people first, and sheen of stripped land up to the edge of the reserve which developers and hunters eye off, their soul's crushed by it just being there for something other than themselves. They will have sway. The orange route, the tear along these lines, Atlantis into the sea, the lines of refugees moving into the dry, waterless inland. Cleared. Uncleared. Clarification. Reclarifying the space for rebuilding in own images. They *fine* their beers with fish bladders and would float in a flooded world. A flooded world without a drop to drink. Nor any drop to drink. Nor any. Drop. To drink. As easy as that, as copyright exists in the textual profit zone but not in the theft of Aboriginal lands. No plagiarism of presence there, eh? And so he wondered, looking at the English magpie on the English green. Gotta love 'em. Love 'em all. Love us. Love me. And there and then, out of love, Harold decided he would disrupt business in any way he could. Any non-violent way. Graffiti. Blocking doorways. Pissing through the cracks. Sab. Love. Sab. Betrayer of Harold but not of foxes. It's okay to love the sab. It is. And to remember. And the orange route up the hill, past Red Hill poison zone, past Gidge to Lillydale, destruction all the way through to Great Eastern Highway, carrying loads east, sucking them in west, and destroying all in the path of lovers' commerce. Job security. Generating wealth. Practicalities. Love in the Antipodes. Too. Love, too. All love, everywhere. Even in the bombing zones world powers have denoted in Syria, or anywhere on the concept of a Middle East—between here and there, there and here. The compass up to its loving tricks. Lovely, this moral compass this search for origins of belief this tracking routes of aspiration this warping to fit the mould this star-crossed lovefest of human ingenuity this denial of difference this love of glory this love of comfort this love of one over another this gameplay in the testing ground that crushed the other into shape to fit the worthiness of your love. Be worthy of my love, it says, And love me as I deserve.

*

I cannot love what I have written, said Harold. I cannot love what I have written because someone else could have written it. And then again, I am happy someone else could have written it, or might write it. Really, that it's written is what matters. Really, I love the text and I love the consequences of text, not its source. I do not own what I have written and make no claim. But now I do not write so I am speaking of the past. I am speaking of the time when I appealed to the actor, my *ex*, and to her friends, but not for what I was writing or what I might write, but the fact that I enacted writing. It showed my other traits as ancillary because writing is an art and art matters—to them, not to me. And that's the problem I had and have. With writing and my love of writing. I would separate writing and reading if I could but I can't. I fall out of love with my reading. So I listen, even when I am reading I am listening to the aural suggestions. A biography of Mahler does this especially. The fifth starts the opposite to how it progresses and we can hear that clearly. I don't need the liner notes. That, they say, Is the beauty of music. I love music but I fear I also love the score, the notes, the bars leaping off the page. I am in awe of a bird's syrinx because of what it can do, what it makes to hear. But my hearing is by no means perfect. My hearing is in decline as my sight is in decline. My love has declined and the residues this decline has left corrode my senses. But in my head, I hear and see and taste as well as I ever did, but so often reject the offerings of these mental sensations. I deny them as I deny love. I am embarrassed by the few possessions I cart around with me. I am embarrassed that people hunt foxes, that they torment and torture animals, that they do it to humans and that they record their doings. Some of them write it. Some of them call it journalism, some of them call it reportage, some of them call it fiction, some of the call it art. I cannot love them though I have abundant love within me.

*

Love is work, says Harold to Harold. Love for men I knew when I was young was language and not practicalities. They were adept at wielding words of control they actually had the gall to think were words of seduction—*seduction* being, they imagined, desired by their targets. Seduction is a form of abuse. Seduction is never love. These tactics they use, lazily, rewriting the past and considering themselves holier than thou when they used and abused—locked their partners in rooms and threatened violence to the restrained or to themselves. If you don't love me, I will self-harm. Harold says to Harold, I have seen it on the fringes of the theatre, I have seen the laziness of lovecraft, the games of seduction, the self-pity they call love. These roles we expect of others, we think we can operate within, getting the work done by others will term significant. Who occupy our thoughts, whom we control to alleviate our needs. All that love without work, that mealy mouthing. But you have loved, Harold, you have. Yes, I have Harold, and known the difference. These phantasms and tropes, these fantastical allusions and registered trademarks. For me, the greatest depravity is the belief in uniqueness and yet, love, real love, can only be unique and specific. Look at the mass claims for the unique love of God or gods or Gods or god.

*

What was it Stendhal wrote in *De l'Amour*? A certain lady in Vienna?

I haven't been there for years, though one day I'd like to hear Mahler's symphonies played in their entirety there.

You have no money to travel.

No. And I am not asking for any. What I most remember from Stendhal about love is the stick in the salt mine near Salzburg. The crystals accruing, the wondrous play of light that is love to our inert selves bringing life. I am hazy today, and I might be misremembering.

It is good to misremember.

Yes, I agree. It is good to misremember. I was fourteen when I was taken to Lake Magic near Wave Rock. The sticks in the lake were encrusted with salt crystals, and minerals and algae entrapped in the latticework disrupted the way even refraction works. Lifted from the lake they dried with threat and joy. It was so hot, the salt on the ground in the dry river bed bubbled. But I walked out into the twists and hooks of deadwood and immediately sunk into sludge, my feet sucked down and my shoes torn off. A thick black silt clung to everything and the miasma of farmkill stunk everything up. I knew about the costs—this is not interpolation—I could see it from the age of eight. I knew the clearing and the fertilising and the toxins deployed to make things grow fast and grow where they weren't suited to grow would cost and bring a stench. But the crystals on the sticks—little barbs and spears and needles and icicles in the surreal heat sliced me up inside as I thought of all the people I'd seen in the world I might have loved but knew I couldn't say a word and what love would await me when I was away from the nurturing, the home that was different from so many homes but a home full of love, a different but potent love, different from the love I envisaged these icy poles of crystals held represented symbolised embodied. Each sliver of love though I know now I know looking back I know remembering in this town of stolen love of theft of body as artefact of love as an anthropological ploy even their own the thieves is that those sticks held the shocked and spiky tears of land and its people and the immensity of presence the landtears showing no deletion is possible no matter how much the colonist bastards try so I come here to confront the collections and the thefts and Euro music playing in my heard disconnected though connected in its own pain its own legacy its own tangents of salt and ice and melt. This failure to understand the love outside myself that had nothing to do with me but to make it all about me is why I flounder and wallow in the cold winds of the fens, the ague in my bones and aged before my time, wanting friends but not knowing how to speak any more and when I do blurting it out, alienating. Stendhal: those people whose awareness of love is delivered via fiction. What of them? Where can they go in an old carved stone town? Victory pleasure ingratiation lack of gratitude the signs of 'intelligence' crystallisation? It's a calling card of oppression. I asked the woman with the child, with the girl who is now refusing school and scratching the new partner and refusing to wash—ever (I understand, I understand . . . I admit, it's five weeks since I bathed, my sheets are grey with dirt, and who am I to judge the cleanliness of another I barely even know . . . though as a child, I was so very very clean . . . scrupulously so)—but memorising Jane Austen novels at the age of . . . what is she . . . nine or ten? . . . I cannot tell. I repeat what is not mine to repeat, the woman with the child who loves the child so much and thinks she loves her new partner who certainly loves her and she confides in me rarely using my name, and I act as intermediary between her and you, her stalker, you who should be, to my mind and I have said it to her, be reported to authorities whom I would normally deplore but you must stop your acts of anti-love of mental torment, you who say you stalk her because it's a connection with 'home' and she denied you and denied your connection to her and consequently 'home'—I reject the notion of the 'expatriate' and I am here to show the lies of the centre of learning the lies of knowledge-gathering the lies of data accumulation of collecting of the theatre of the gown where love is an examination in which the better studied will do better even when their 'hearts' are left pickled in labs and sold to private companies on the town's edge. Collaborations of love. The child rejects the town rejects people but loves the text loves the Austen world and the ducks and plunges on into life like no one else matters, but loves her mother to the point of obsession and fears a life growing up without her. I understand. I understand. I respect. She sees. She thinks you are a ghost a ghoul a doppelganger a trick of the light. She doesn't like the heat of Australia, that's all she'll say. She says you are like the heat reflecting off glass off the pavement she remembers walking to a shop with her mother as a toddler, being picked up because it's too hot and shiny and she only has little legs. But she remembers magpies with sharp beaks and she loved their song and she knows the magpies of Cambridge are different from the magpies of where she comes from. She knows you, *Stalker*, are the opposite of love, that you destroy love. She knows her mother's new partner loves her mother and she also fears that, and she disrupts, but she knows *you* are all that love is not. She has your measure. She is watching you. You will not grow in her presence or at her expense. And I am watching you, too.

You amuse me. And that girl tells lies. I hear them. I respect them. She lies just as your beloved Sab Woman lies.

I cannot pay for this tea, I have no money.

No problem, it's on me, as always.

*

I prefer animals to humans—I mean, I prefer non-human animals.

Yes. That's fine. You are always covered in cat fur.

Rescue cats. I feed them a vegan substitute. I put bells around their necks to warn the birds.

I like you, Sab Woman, but I could never love you, not really. I am not sure why you come around so much. Is it pity?

Why should I pity you?

I don't know. I had an aviary when I was child. For a few

years when we were living in Narrogin. I kept birds trapped on farms. They weren't happy, I could tell, but I never let them go. I loved them, in my own way. I wanted them to be happy though there wasn't enough room for them to fly. There were quail at the bottom of the aviary, running around and digging at the dirt floor, and them seemed happier. But they probably weren't. I had no friends at school so they were my friends. If I'd had friends at school I might have let them all go. Maybe, maybe not.

I grew up on a fur farm. When I was fourteen I cut a hole in the security fence with boltcutters, then opened the cages, and let the mink free. They devastated the countryside. My punishment was to have the damage they did rubbed into my soul. I was called a murderer and an environmental vandal. The mink were hunted and slaughtered. But as I suffered, I found in my action a purpose, and something more generous than the hypocrites who raised me who loved me who taught me their morality.

Do we intersect, Sab Woman? Is there enough commonground? I do not want to sleep with you. I don't want to sleep with anyone. I have no desire.

Love can be independent of the physical.

Yep, I agree. In fact, love has nothing to do with the body as far as I am concerned. But if I'd even heard that twenty years ago I would have laughed in the face of the speaker.

Sometimes it's good to hear a human voice, just sounds coming out and adding up to a sharing.

I am feeling that might be true, but tomorrow I might go back to my silence. I don't know. It's not a fickle thing—I just don't know. When the urge for silence comes I can't control it. Speech shuts down for me. At times. And when it has shutdown I think it will never come back.

Stendhal: Constancy, intimacy . . .

You've been reading that? Good. Strikes me that the thing is to read it against the grain, muddle it up in your head. Rework it. The Italian women listening to love and music for six hours a day. Can you imagine.

No. It doesn't translate.

Is that a Brexit response? There's a subtext of Brexiteering in the animal rights movement.

You mean an English (say say say) equivalent of Bridget Bardot's Front National anti-Islamic animal rights hate stuff? A confusion of values. I oppose linkages between human cultures and the exploitation of animals. I am more nuanced than you think me. Or like to think me.

Maybe I want to avoid the risk of love—the more nuanced, the more entangled, the more tautological, the more at risk I am. An exposure to love is not what I want. I want to finish the Mahler biography. I want to listen to his fifth without risk, without irony, with the bulk of it washing over me and just being. I don't want to explain. It troubles my head. I am a recovering addict. I have to prioritise and find my places of retreat.

Music is more than that, surely. How can you say this stuff? I mean, it's bullshit and you know it. You come and help sabotage the hunts, but you're always at one remove. You listen to music with an impassive, even blank look on your face like you feel nothing. You drink tea and eat just enough. How do you earn a living, what do you like off? How do you pay your rent? There's nothing there, no information, no reality. You talk sometimes, and sometimes a lot. Then you're silent. You cannot stand people touching you and you never touch other people. Music doesn't exist in you or you kill it off before it can set root. And yet you say Mahler matters to you more than anything else. But it's as if there's no Mahler in you, and that Mahler has no effect on you. It's just something you say.

Sure, I am in denial. What of it? I would like you to leave now and let me return to my blankness. Thankyou.

Symphony No. 6

Mahler's 6th in Perth

The wealthy poison trees along the foreshore
To widen and intensify their view of skyscrapers—
Stretch of the river mediating business.
In the Concert Hall Mahler's 6th is going off.

The residual lakes of once great wetlands
Condensed to edges, walkways, mowable
Green strips, demi-nurture an array of water-

Birds. Stilled on the bank of little Lake Tondut
Is the nankeen night heron, modulating
Intactness and a defiant metaphysics of snare.

As day is to the massing of instruments,
As night to the brazen trumpet, frenetic
Triangle, and the hammer blows we won't
Call tragic—never tempting a third strike.

*

I am not conflating but I can't help that it rushes back in, fills the blank, then there's the promise of what's to come, which, in this Brexit zeitgeist, is not good. I see those 'little' racist acts being gotten away with in the streets, especially on the train, especially in London. And now I hear Sab Woman has lost her mother, the fur-farm proprietor (her father having divorced and remarried and gone into a burger franchise). The fur farm has been willed to the Sab Woman.

*

Harold squeezed between bikes near the door so he could stumble out as soon as the train pulled into King's Cross. The healthy aggressive cyclist closest to him was also ready to make a break for it, having a sip from his water bottle, then clipping it back on the bike frame. Helmeted, he said to Harold, Where are you from? You're an odd *colour*—is that jaundice or ethnic? Those were his precise words. Harold ignored him, though it sunk in, sank to the place all such things sank in Harold. Harold's grandfather had said to him, When we fought the Japs in New Guinea all my mates gave them the usual racist names. But that's not the way. An enemy is something the state assigns you—as those soldiers were assigned their fate by their governments, by the greedy powers-that-be in their own culture. And even the dreadful individuals were created as dreadful by the mechanisms of their family, their state, the manipulation of their culture to further the interests of the powers-that-be, of which their emperor was the ultimate symbol, the manifestation of the divine rights of kings which has extended across the planet in the control of the many by the few. Harold's grandfather was a radical, according to Harold's father. But Harold's father saw radicals everywhere, and in fact abandoned Harold and his mother because of her 'hippy tendencies' . . . he wanted to make the best of what God offered and to suck the country dry and purchase a decent car and to indulge himself as he so desired. Which he did. But Harold wasn't giving room to any of that. Further, his Dad's other children weren't 'decent'. There was a lost brother. There was a half-sister. And she loathed her father and left him and her mother whenever the opportunity arose and though she burnt things down and wrecked their house preferred being with Harold's hippy mum (who wasn't in the slightest hippy) and Harold, showing him her privates which she said will warp him for the rest of his life which was her plan—she said, it's up to me to create the vengeance. She loved the word vengeance. But Harold's grandfather said the Japs were people and their cruelty was a reflection of the cruelty that had created the idea of power and war in the first place, and that many of the soldiers he fought with as mates were as cruel whenever they could get away with it and the state had its ways of allowing them to get away with it.

At the front of the station Harold heard the police yelling before he saw them. They were nearby and pushing a man with a backpack to the ground and pushing automatic weapons into his back and his face and trying to separate the backpack from the man's back and to isolate it and cover it with something flexible but impervious. Was that how it was? Harold knew he was relying on what he'd seen elsewhere and in news reports and in movies when he'd watched them with his ex- seducing an enemy of the state to extract vital information. But it was happening in realtime and then he realised the man wasn't a man but a young woman and her face was covered then uncovered and she was screaming words that Harold felt had nothing to do with God so he deleted them as they fed into his ears which were full of the 6th. The irony and repulsiveness of this made him vomit green bile because as usual he hadn't eaten that morning. The bike man was nearby watching on as police arrived more and more pushing back and saying clear the area. The bike man was having another drink and saying racist things and wishing vengeance and death, pushed back on his wheels, as the bomb squad came into play in a full-on kind of way and Harold was nowhere or not where he was or thought he was because it was lockdown and lock-out time. The state was clicking into gear and antibodies were at work and the distressed woman was muzzled and carted off and her backpack was vanished and time hiccupped and phone cameras were making the truth of here & now. The 6th was strangely jaunty, hopping about towards those *hammer blows* of driving the point home. The bang bangs the tragic bang bang the kids' trumpets in the hallways of the BNP the protest against the flow of propriety the irony of 'orator's blows' of nothingness to fill in their own earspace their own biographies this acid in the face this protest against effusions beautiful and exquisite and enriching and complex and contradictory and as it should be growths of diversity of hearing and seeing and knowing different exchange at the crisis of confrontation of fate banging on and they don't get the desire for relevance of presence in all places one is where are they are theirs ours we it you I and all in the set-subset busting out and a rainbow across the sheen of his eyes as down as down incidental but down kicked by fascists down and an insight of what would come must come fatally God fatally. Harold suddenly loved Mahler and knew his loves and pains and struggles with the conservatives, the rightwing press. Was this it? Who was it? Or was he losing his hold on events. He slipped, beaten.

*

How did Harold end up at the Earl's house in Kensington? How did he go from the gardens to the house, how did the bloom of an out-of-season flower end up in his jacket buttonhole? How did he get sprayed with perfume as he walked down the hall to the drawing room? The Earl was on the board of Sellafield and wanted to pick Harold's brains about all this protest rot. After all, his name had been mentioned at an A-list party just recently. Is it true, Sir, that you were once the partner of the Great Actress (he said Actress), Lucida, and that you had a child together that died in infancy. Harold stared at the monster, and at his surroundings, and asked, How did you find me? There was an incident outside King's Cross. You were there, Sir? You were a witness. Harold felt like he was going to cry. He felt grateful that he was about to cry and be embarrassed. His loathing for The Earl was rejuvenating. He knew what he loathed and why he loathed it. He was offered tea in bone china, he was offered, believe it or not, some madeleine on a silver platter. The Earl said, Nuclear waste is the future—the wealth of the nation, processing it. Australia will be getting in on the act very soon I have it on good authority. The Earl stank of the atomic tests at Maralinga—he was a carcinogen.

*

Harold's reading was a not a success. He lost his way trying to recite from memory because he held the pages in front of him and got distracted by the text. He repeated himself not as refrain, but because he'd forgotten where he was. He dribbled. He shook. He tried to sing 'Twist and Shout' but it came out as a mutter and the intense young people in the front rows laughed, but not in a kind way. Then during the interval which for Harold became the end of the reading because he slipped out, but not before one of the intense young things who was studying *Everyman* and writing a new critical apparatus for a new publishing house who would not publish online but only on de-acidified archival paper that would last a thousand years (or so they said, or so Harold thought they said), asked him if he knew Kate Moss and if she would come and speak to their Group. Who is Kate Moss? asked Harold, clutching his poems, then he was gone.

*

Harold listened intently to the ricochet at the end of the vinyl recording of the 6th stuck in its end-groove, going on for as long as power from the nuclear reactors fed it. He wondered if he was short-changing The Earl whom he could not really remember—had he picked him up in the park? Really. Was he a mature man with distinguished grey hair? Was it a Saville Row suit? Was he impeccable? Was he tall? Was he thin? Did he have a driver? Was it a Jaguar with leather seats that made Harold squirm with guilt? Suggestive gyrations? I do not do sex, said Harold. Not in any size shape or form. I have no objections to you performing sex on yourself, but I don't do sex. What was the actress like in bed? She hasn't aged, has she? Can afford not to age. I hear she's going to be cryogenically frozen before she gets too old. She's still getting roles, isn't she? You can't be as old as you look. Spruce yourself up a bit mean—this old boho look isn't becoming. No, not at all. And you smell bad. Ricochet—shrapnel—a jackhammer in the street outside. Hammer blows of fate. The Queen Anne furniture of the drawing room squirmed under his broken fingernails. It's all adjectives and exaggeration, he thought. Loss makes everything else comic. What can they do to me, really? Ricochet ricochet. Listening to the groove eat itself, he started reciting *The Prelude* in his head. He would keep going until book after book took him to the end. It was all in there. There was no escaping it. Retribution. He had no other cultural referents to call upon, and in the house of imperialism he was bereft.

*

To drink that first milk. Colostrum. To drink the cheesy milk. To gain sight over the days of reawakening—the second awakening after the amniotic flow, the massiveness of a liquid world. The senses flooding in, mediated, then not, but the nipple the connector to all that will follow. But Harold could not move on from the loss. The suddenness. Her pain was so great she forgot every line she'd ever learned. What they shared was dreadful—what followed could only be ephemeral and she grabbed it entire. The shallow world would be replicated shallower in her acting, in her embracing of its absurdity. Her father's wealth and power that made a hole and absence of her mother couldn't intervene to stop the stopping of the breathing of the sucking on the nipple of the heart. There's no getting over and no iron mountain decapitated and shunted off in railway wagons and ships and into furnaces and recast as cars coming back to clot the streets and airways could make a difference. The blame: must have been a result of the shit he ingested of the fumes his sperm gave off, the better half worsted. But that would also admit defeat. We cannot ever sidestep the total loss of innocence the child of Plato in the fading lightbulb of modernity. Six months of silence and then obliteration of everything, and a glamorous rising into product placement and yellow-haired racial profiling and cheekbones working and lips shaping and those intonations of a girl's private school after the 'rough edges' (her father's words) of the state schools working outwards to all private schools of the world and those two years in a finishing school in Switzerland finally paying off (her father's words) and a way through the trauma the loss as brutal as the accolades that stack the emptiness.

*

It was warming then raining more. It seemed only last week it had snowed. He had slipped on black ice and hurt his tailbone. He saw the woman and the child and the woman's partner and went up to say hello but they all turned away like they didn't know him. It was cold and he was hot with shame. Normally, he would turn away, that was the defence, but now he was feeling the shame and a loneliness he'd forgotten. He went and knocked on Shakespeare's door looking for company, but Shakespeare only opened the door a crack and warned Harold away, I am really sick, my fellow. You don't want to come in here. But he did—he didn't care if it was fatal. It was warming then raining more. Not much time had passed, and yet the weather was shifting fast, too fast. There were mosquitoes and summer birds appeared in his sleep, which was restless. The mildew was deep in his lungs. But it was months now since he'd moved to the house in the fields. So, why was he back in the basement listening to Shakespeare hack his guts up? Two places at once, two seasons at once. He had lost track.

*

Prayer to nowhere and no one and only in daylight hours. In the light. On a bench, hunched over, his coat drawn around his neck in winter or summer, Harold was praying. A steady mumble in his head, the dreaded violins which he also loved hacking away at his solemnity with their solemnity. When praying he found that he was attractive to robins. Though a different species, as a teenager in the Western Australian wheatbelt, red-capped robins had come to him when he stared into oblivion, across the stubble to the aching white-walled dam in extreme heat. That was when he learned to pray. Once with her—with his ex-, mother of his deceased offspring [even though there was no biological question to be asked, he asked the question of the possessive 'his': by what right, really?]—with Lucida—who had just triumphed (again) as Ophelia in a production at the Playhouse, Perth[3]—one with *her*, he said, We all pray

[3] Harold first experienced Mozart's *Don Giovanni* on the stage, under the arch, with Lucida not long after the renovation of His Majesty's Theatre in Perth, Western Australia. He wanted to join the musicians in the pit, but he was drawn to the stage, and was eventually struck by the lightning. I am a peasant, he whispered to Lucida who shushed him. After the performance, both of them walked out into Hay Street in a stupor before nearly being struck by a car and snapping out of it. That theatre was built by filthy gold money, said Harold. I love it, said Lucida, and I love to hate the Don. Harold argued for Donna Elvira, whom he understood via the 'murder' the Don had done unto her. But Lucida was not going to let Harold take that line as his own, and wrested it from him. We will have sex for 1,003 days in a row, she said, Not necessarily with each other. I do not want to have sex with anyone but you, Lucida. When the Armada was blown off course, she said, a Spanish sailor found one of my ancestors on an Irish headland and I become part of the story. I have a responsibility. Harold knew the word 'destiny' was about to be deployed so he wrapped his arms around her and said, Let's get out of the city—the crops are drying off and the air will be heady up beyond The Hills. Let's go and think over our hearing and our experience tonight. Let's be near the harvest. The weddings? asked Lucida, mockingly. And with that, Harold knew Lucida was set on another course, and that for 1,003 nights he would be celibate and would hear the minuet playing over and over in his unsleeping head. He knew he was not going to sleep for 1,003 days and nights. He knew that the costs of seduction would sour his food and drink, and that the grinding props of crop dusters sweeping the crops and poisoning the world, the flames of fire summers, the volleys of sporty gunfire would frame his reality and gradually the arias would fall away. He would write a book, a book of names as recited by Lucida of all her conquests. She had to set an example, she had to change the discourse, and he, Harold, understood this, of course. Of course. How long was this before Lucida's first starring role—could we say Ophelia at the Playhouse was her breakout moment? How old were they when they met? They had met when they were at high school—schools far apart in different topographies. Maybe they met at the movies, where they happened to be, away from their schools the patterns of their lives? Harold would be taking notes—he always took notes. A little pocketbook of scribbles in the flashy light, the soundtrack shade. This girl, who says, I won't be anything you want me to be. I am not made to be remade by you or anybody. I act to confirm myself, not to 'be in character'. He regretted taking those last-minute tickets to *Don*

to pronouns. One way or another. She punched him in the arm, and it hurt his soul. Prayer is despair! she said. She was fond of a first violinist in one of the major Australian orchestras at the time, and did the mini violin thing for

---

Giovanni—the seats not the best and it being a spur of the moment thing. And the money to purchase them had come from somewhere but where? Neither of them spoke Italian at that point (or stage), but each of them understood every word as it was sung. They understood the words deeper than they would have understood English. Harold was confused about ancestry and baulked as Lucida who usually disowned all parentage and heritage said, Blood runs deeper . . . It sounded like a promo for a show, a bloody show he wasn't going to be part of. But Harold ruminated over his pushing the issue so long ago, We must go, we must go . . . did you know that Mahler did a production in New York on January 23rd, 1908 at the MET (he said Met with such confidence at the time . . . and now it made him cringe further into the bright coldness of *The Winter's Tale* which he was rereading so he could talk it over with his friend . . . or is this out of synch with his chronology, his biography, he wonders . . . And, he said excitedly to a bored and sceptical Lucida who was pushing to do something different on that (fateful) might was pushing to go hotel-crash the rooms of a visiting one-hit wonder band for a zine she was running, but Harold had shifted the tempo of the discussion by saying (with gravitas, enthusiasm and authority . . . and all seduction he was capable of mustering), I have a copy of the *New York Times* review (he said at the time: NYT review) of the performance . . . I have it memorised . . . and he quoted this paragraph as raison d'être: 'Much was expected of Mr. Mahler's direction of the performance, which he controlled and dominated with results that were in many ways admirable. The most significant feature of it was in the matter of tempi, which in several places differed from what lovers of Mozart's masterpiece here are accustomed to. Some of his tempos were hastened, some were kept back; thus, in the duet between Don Giovanni and Zerlina, the "la ci darem" was quicker that it is usually taken, and the succeeding "Andiamo" much slower-and the result in this case as in some others, did not carry conviction.' [https://www.gustav- mahler.eu/index.php/plaatsen/145-america/new-york-city/2997-1908-opera-new- york-23-01-1908] Lucida! It 'differed' . . . the performance 'differed' . . . exclaimed a jubilant and persuasive Harold. The rubbing off of enthusiasm always carries consequences and will be resented. He imagined he'd thought this at the time, but he hadn't. But he was determined he'd remain committed to the course of resistance for 1,003 days at least. I can stay alive that long. I can be relied on. I will watch over the sabs from this lifeless shell. Living inside the death-coating. Or dead inside the fleshy occupation of space. Not here with memory lying to me about past performances, always eager to hear, to watch, to experience. He began a list of every Mahler performance seen and heard. Each anomaly, variation, liberty. He had experienced 1,003 of them, without any numerical superstition. In his withering, he pursued the distant thought of one more, to break the hoodoo, to open a path beyond the seduction of the show. Dwelling alone, hearing the dirty plumbing straining to take the wastes of semi-strangers away, the flushing through to the bright sparks of Hell, the rolling away of the day's digestions as asbestos-skins ignore/d the lapping (of) flames. This cauldron we inhabit, he thought he thinks he (mis)remembers. The rubbish bin and punishment and the swamp and the crops of far far away I would call home if I could. *Don Giovanni* at The Maj.

mocking pity as his lip turned down. Why do you never use my name? she asked. I mean, it's ridiculous. We should marry, he said. Don't be ABSURD, said she.

Prayer in the blinding light, head down. He mused that many of the deeply religious people he'd known were only a prayer away from a loss of self-control. Why could he not believe? Why did he look into churches and temples and mosques and try to find a place for himself? Why did he try to reconstruct the church of his childhood in his head? There were two: a country church with stretched kangaroo windows that shed a violently soothing light on roo shooters, and a suburban church in which an equally modernist window ate the setting sun but was suppressed at morning service. That suburban church with its open spaces and liberated high church contradiction. Kneeling, he pretended to pray. Now, in the open light of day on a bench he hunched and prayed all the way into oblivion.

Once, up a tower, maybe of Notre Dame, he'd looked out over the iconising of ordinary life, of pleasure and suffering, and thought, here I am supposed to feel elevated because of the architecture and passage of time. But out in the arid places of childhood I felt an immensity and fullness that scared and excited me. But then I realised what had been built into me to receive it in such away, and it was shut off from me forever. I had to leave, but by bit. Praying helps me go away, the Yellow Brick Road collapsing and falling away with each step, never to be retraced.

There was a man who wanted to mentor manliness in him when his father went. Was gone. The man had a gun safe and he said, I keep my prayers in there.

Harold's prayers were often interrupted by curious police officers. What are you doing? Why are you hanging around here? Do you have a fixed address? And sometimes by social workers wanting to feed him, offer him shelter, which he didn't take as an insult but appreciated. On five occasions he had been arrested while praying, but always released without charge. He had a record from his druggy youth in Australia, but it hadn't caught up with him in any meaningful way. He still crossed borders, sometimes walking over them sans passport. Just to be on the other side, not to recognise the divide, though he wished no disrespect on cultural differences. In this he became confused, as he did watching the big screen in the theatre—dazzled by the obscene size of people when taken away from his being physically close to them. I am separated off, he prayed. Sitting and praying his haemorrhoids bothered him. He hated shitting in public toilets but rarely shat anywhere else. He relied on public conveniences. He always cleaned up after himself and gave the toilet a brush if there was a brush nearby. He cleaned his sore bum well, but didn't care about much else on his body. Once, he rarely got infections or sick, but now it was different. A cut on the back of his hand was festering. He prayed around it. He got it while out sabbing, and the Sab Woman tried to clean it up, but it really made no difference. He said, The rot of the hunters has found its way in, and it's likely fatal. They are a pestilence. I agree, said the Sab Woman, But that's all the more reason to heal thyself. I will pray for you, she said, which made him cock a grey eyebrow because she was a pagan to her friends and a heathen to her enemies—he wondered to whom or what she might praying. He hoped a tree. Harold had always loved trees, especially the forest. It was hard to find much forest in Britain outside plantation forest. He liked ancient forest and felt an affinity with moss—clumps of moss. He would sometimes weep seeing moss fallen from steep slates in Cambridge streets. The loss. The loss. Prayer was inevitably tragic in its ending because an end is inevitable. You cannot sustain a permanent stream of prayer, though churches keep people to do so—in shifts. To keep the energy beam happening, to keep the channel open with strength. So they think, so they think, he thought.

Symphony No. 7

Night. The barn owl is watching. The barn owl in the fens. The barn owl on the edge of the Victoria Plains, wheatbelt Western Australia. The barn owl outside imperialist language. The barn owl disturbed in its scanning by the heavy thud of woofers across the valley. The claimants are partying loud. V8 utes are doing burnouts—gravel to bitumen. So what do you do, Harold, thinking about her who has left you to go east to make her first full-length movie? Who has been 'discovered'? The night sky is alive with brilliantine stars. Paste. Zirconia suspended. Harold knows the owl is nearby, astounded but unreceptive in the risen and collapsed and rerouted and risen York gum below the house. He is alone with the barn owl and the rodents and the roosting birds vulnerable in the starlight and the thumping music of a big stereo and the freedom rituals the bacchic enactments across the valley, the dry winter creek running adrenaline and threat, the granites emanating their old radiation and insects rustling towards the artificial lights. Harold turns up the portable stereo on which he is listening to the 7th. It can barely yell back to the dance music, the partiers unable to hear over their own utterances, own channellings. But Harold feels vindicated then guilty and turns it down and then off and lets night fill him in and the barn owl move towards him, towards lights out under stars, rodents tracking across the ceiling, the verandah taking it all in.

Night. They would go out when she wasn't working and he wasn't writing or studying and see whatever was on in city movie theatres. Anything at all. Just to sit and watch in company. But not a social act, caught up as they were, saturated in screenlight, occasionally lapsing into the exit signs, the green or red sideshow. They never ate in the theatre, they never spoke to each other, they leaned towards each other in order not to lean towards others, but rarely touched intentionally. As soon as they left the theatre they would find a bar or coffee house and sit for an hour or two and talk the movie through in every way they could think of. They never went to matinées. It only worked at night, knowing the dark or quasi-dark of the theatre was enclosed in the quasi-dark of the suburb or city, that beyond them that part of the world was inside darkness, away from the sun.

Night. She was wary of the country, of being beyond the artificial halo that hung over the city even in the early hours of the morning. Her father had taken her up to the mines as a small girl and she stayed in the huts, fearing the machinery hacking away at the earth under floodlights all night long, the bottom of the pit filling with water where there was no rain. He had said, Be careful of stepping on snakes at night—they're out in the warm, hunting for mice.

She wasn't scared of the snakes, but she was scared of the night out where the earth was being eaten. She said this to Harold in one of her 'weaker moments', and regretted and denied it almost immediately. You love the night *out there*, she said, It's not natural—and it makes you more of an alien than you think. She said that, she who on the screen betrays a face and body 'without work' that Harold knows deep in his flesh is made up, is sculpted and injected and remodelled in the image of desire, of persistence against the cultural normatives. Silver screen. Windscreen at night. Roos on the road. The mining trucks hauling the earth to find the blast furnaces to find the forms that will make movies, streamed and there and out in the night of a country closed and closing in, lip-service to whose country it is transformed into consumables so it is a universal loss sold as gain.

Night. Klaxons. Rousing up the lights-off houses of isolation. Revving engines and furious stereos. Spotlights and shots fired. It happened to Harold as a child, he and his mother hunching and crouching and shivering behind the shed, next to the pepper tree smelling of damp hessian nailed galvanised nails pinioning hessian to the tree a slung a cubby and chook scratchings making a rocky foothold and chickenpoop smell all uric fear as the utes circled and into the dark house shots were fired and a hooting and hollering drunken victory call and a rape threat yelled even by a girl who was seventeen and out with the boys and they knew they all knew and shaking together gripping hard arm to arm till gone and mother saying they hide behind the accusations that we with our victim mentalities create clichés and stereotypes of them the boys and their girls who they will rape and beat and it will be decades before the women can and will speak and by then the victims beyond themselves for they are victims deep victims too perpetrator victims we the victims of now will be long gone as everyone knows the country isn't really like that for they drive us out at night and we survive into the day if we're lucky and make arrangements to leave and never come back Harold never come back. The night is sacred but they think it is *their* opening their gawping mouths to suck it in and let it back out thinking they possess it all and middle-class academic boys and girls will reclaim their rights through text and image and say the ute boys are hard done by and that icons always cop it tough and victims are them and they need rights and a national poet will rise and wear his hat and speak the lingo and claim the uteboys for himself and the world will welcome the authentic the true voice of the bush. Beware, Harold beware the poet who wants the brightlights and says he knows the nights, all humble and ordinary and bush and watching the game and knowing the airline schedules and plotting ways to overcome jetlag, shifts from day to night to day all in one flight, and then another and another.

*

Yes, it's possible—maybe even a fact—that the ute drivers might change over time, regret their actions. There may even be more to them than the tooled boots that hold them upright when they sway, the stetson or akubra that gives them thought-power that allows their patriotism to shine, to emanate out through the Southern Cross, reinforce the

Union Jack, that's true—and the ups & downs of life, the trauma of loss sincerely felt, even tears over the loss of a prized pig dog, a dog raised from a pup, a vicarious sharer of bushkill experiences, and even a flutter of love, yes love, in the chest where the heartbeat shakes with sexual buzz. All of it is true, no one-dimensional take on the ute drivers surrounding, attacking the dark house at night. But at the moment of fear, at the moment of susceptibility. And from the point of view of the mother and child, shaking with a fear that is a fear come of war, that's as the case may be. You don't like it in your narratives because narratives are space and time and you want to use yours for a variety of read experiences. No clotting the airwaves of more of the same. *A Fistful of Dollars*—in fact, the whole trilogy—did it for you. Travels and rises like prophecy on the screens of Australia. That'll do, mate, that'll do. Sensitive readers you all. You judges, you narrowers of experience making life fuller for your effetes (the irony—live out there and maintain your values without subterfuge and see how long before the utes arrive to straighten you out). But in the dormitory suburbs, the same whispers and whisperers. The killing rooms of the everyday. Sometimes the bitterness swept over Harold. He fought through to daylight so he could pray.

*

Night. The brightest time of day. Thanks for chatting with me. Would you like something to eat? You seem never to eat. What good fortune to stumble across you like that. I searched for you at the house of the basement, and I searched for you at the house in the field, and you were nowhere. Where have you been? Where are you living?

In London. Sleeping rough.

Funny expression, isn't it, sleeping rough. I mean I toss and turn all night, and always look worse for wear in the morning. And you only—excuse me—look worse for wear. So, cup of tea?

Thankyou.

Okay, tea for you and a pasta dish with a glass of house red for me.

You still stalking the woman with the child?

Oh, not really—been searching for the ghost of myself. I am guessing you've lost contact with the woman yourself.

I am not interested in anyone.

Did you have an imaginary friend as a child?

No. I talked to myself—I was my own imaginary friend.

Quite. I can see that. Well I had one and it is still with me. I am being stalked by my imaginary friend. I guess you've never got away from your imaginary friend either. Maybe we can help each other with . . . techniques?

If I didn't want myself to be understood I spoke in a language only I knew.

It is always good to have a secret language, but isn't it usually shared? I certainly share it with my ghost. My ghost is no hip American ghost that opens the possibility of spontaneity in the absorption of American society, though it first appeared there—left off the silver screen during a double matinee feature. I was living in Phoenix with my parents who were speculating in land using what was left of the family fortune. Anyway, that's by the by and I take my storylines from elsewhere—though I will say they're from real life as that's what I do, watch people in realtime in real-life in the here and now... none of it is speculative, really . . . I never know what the next moment will bring, how I will react. A pot of green tea? I do believe it's Fair Trade. Ethical tea.

Tea is rarely ethical drunk in the UK. It's a contradiction in terms.

Anyway, I am trying to rid myself of myself. Any suggestions? asks the Stalker.

I would like to go. Thanks for the offer of tea. I don't like the nights to be so bright. I like them to be dark. I don't want you close to me. I don't want you following me. I don't want to be here, but I have no way back.

No. No way back. Back. No, you go . . . off with you, wander away. I am just passing the time. I grow bored very easily. I think I will wine & dine solo. I think I'll take in a movie at the Arts later. I hear *Rage* is getting good notices. Have you caught it? They say your ex- actually really does the sex scenes—you know, no body doubles and no bits of silicon faux body parts in-between. Skin and hair and fluid. A radical move for an *older woman*. Proud of her body, as I've heard she should be. Fit. Well, see you. Catch you around . . . sleep tight, don't let the bed bugs . . . bite! Sleep under a willow tree along the banks of the Cam! That'll help! You might get a free taste or a drink or something. Don't do such things anymore? You're struggling with that door, aren't you—infernal bells—Ms. Ms. . . . yes you, would you help that old gentleman out into the street? He's struggling. Goodnight, old man! Be seeing you!

*

Night. There are plenty of good people out there, but most are sleeping. Though it's morning 'back home' that can't be home, and plenty of good people are getting ready to go to work, are kissing their partners, hugging their parents, smiling at the magpies on the lawn. Plenty of good people all over the globe sleeping and waking and walking and crying and taking last breaths. All of it. Plenty of good people in country towns in isolated places. Plenty. Night. Not holier than thou. Never suggested. Know glasshouses, I am pierced with thousands of splinters. The shattered self. Night.

*

Harold woke in Shakespeare Man's room. Shakespeare [man] was coughing and reading. He looked up over his glasses at the bundle on his couch and said, You weren't very coherent when I found you at the front door. Your basement room has been cleared out. But there wasn't much in there—I guess you took it across to the house in the field. They don't want you back here. But you can stay on the couch for a couple of days. What's mine is yours . . . And Harold stirred and interrupted with a sickish laugh, And what's yours is mine . . . ? Ha. But thank you. I remember now—the night got the better of me, I was drawn to the light of the glass front door, of memory. Of bloody Mahler playing on that old phonograph all night? Yes, that, too. Thank you—it's kind of you to take me in. Well, you don't look so good, old man. I'm okay now. Good to hear. Shakespeare coughed hard, then spluttered, Would you like a cuppa. Tea? That'd be lovely, thanks.

*

Some bastard was shooting at rooks with an ancient rifle. An old gun he called his 'childhood girlfriend'. He said, We used to shoot hundreds of them, knocking over their rookeries.

It would have been a rook gun, said Harold.

You know about such things? the Sab woman asked, distressed.

Sadly, I do. And the crow came to Isaiah and fed him fruit in his crevice.

Sorry?

Nothing, just my trappedness. Before I left Australia I lived briefly on the neck of The Scarp near an orchard. An old bastard paid a young bastard to shoot white-tailed and red-tailed black cockatoos when they alighted on his orchard. They are a protected species, but that didn't matter to them. People objected but fearing the old man and the young man they said nothing. I confronted them and was shot in the foot by a .22. It went through the side of my sandshoe and grazed my instep. It infected. I was off my feet for weeks. No charges were laid, it was called an accident. Along with my grandfather, I am the only person in three generations to receive a bullet wound. So far as I know. So far. Rook guns were kids guns in many ways—but lethal. Smooth-bore horrors of the woods and fields. Deadly pop guns. When the black cockatoos came in great numbers it was night in day, but now their flocks are so thinned it's like a reminder of night, a night that might never come. They can barely carry the weight of the day's shadows now.

You really are a weird man, Harold—you seem to have a lot of difficulty separating the comic and the tragic. I don't know what to believe or what to take seriously.

I am always serious. I am never *comic*. Though I recognise people see me as a comic figure. Someone to be laughed at, rather than laughed with.

Oh, don't take offence. Gee, you can wallow in self-pity. I don't think I've ever heard you laugh!

Oh, I laugh, just not in public. I suppose it's a matter of what you find funny. I mean, animal cruelty humour wouldn't tickle your funny bone, would it!?

Nor yours, I'd imagine.

That's obvious. But I am not selling humour as a survival kit—you are.

I don't find things funny that come at the expense of something or someone else.

Unless it's me? I don't count?

You're wallowing again. Wallowing in your own darkness.

Darkness is a positive as far as I am concerned, Sab Woman. Night is always with me. Night is existence's saving grace. Night is the time beyond prayer. Night renounces the dominance of the sun, which has us in its thrall. A moonless night is the ultimate truth. Without the moon's ironic gaze we declare ourselves.

I love the moon. A full moon showing as many features as we are willing to see.

Night doesn't rely on the eyes, on insight. Night is inside

us—the building block.

Would you like to sleep over at my place tonight—you seem unanchored at the moment.

No thanks. I am staying with Shakespeare. I am learning from him. He is dying but doesn't care. Instead of quizzing me about who I am and where I come from, he has allotted me a text, which he says does the job. And I can accept that:

> Give me my Romeo; and, when I shall die,
> Take him and cut him out in little stars,
> And he will make the face of heaven so fine
> That all the world will be in love with night
> And pay no worship to the garish sun.

Touché!

*

Let daylight flood in to write about night. Let the traces of possum movements, the infinitesimal heat-traces of geckoes' feet on walls show where they tracked, let the feather of a nightjar draw the nightcalls out into the morning. This is where he is, on the couch, sack of poor potatoes, sack of unbelonging, curled up bursting to piss, Shakespeare out early, somewhere in the streets, maybe standing on the picket lines protesting the gargantuan greed of the university taking the old ages away from workers, the insecurity of Brexiteering Britain. He is thinking the wheatbelt while he is listening to a tit sing outside the window—so different-sounding from down in the basement. A morning sound he fuses with nightthoughts. In London—when was it, last week?—he had walked (he didn't march) with the group protesting racism—and had been jostled by short-headed whites, some of whom yelled in his face and threatened to spray him with acid. That'd get a reaction! said one to his imperviousness. Another said, It makes me sick seeing you close to our monuments. You mean the Wrens? asked Harold, and got snotted. And as he fell, he said, I will always be Irish you little shits, and I detest nation and your stinking Eng-a-land! Then fuck off back home to wherever it is you come from. And the horror went into Harold's hollowed guts because he'd pretty well stopped eating. He was a breatharian, a smog-eater of London, a London Fog merchant in his coat, silly old fucker, Irish pig pretending to be a white pretending to be all chummy across the Oirish Sea, fucker. One of the kickers was wearing A Sex Pistols t-shirt and another was wearing a Joy Division t-shirt. Facts, go and unravel that apologists. But then, it should be forgotten, that hanging back watching on, watching his shaved-headed disciples, was The Earl. London is a small town really. The Earl was dressed in a suit but instead of a t-shirt was wearing a Chelsea football club t-shirt. Harold's eye swelled and darkness came down, day-night. Chelsea supporters were the most racist, he recalled, followed by Leeds supporters and Manchester United supporters. He made a mantra of this as he fell entirely to night, left prayer behind. Facts. Truth. Details that upset the joys of any narrative, the entertaining curve of textual travel.

*

Shakespeare gave Harold twenty quid for tidying the room. Harold did a good job. They ate beans on toast and read *Double Falsehood* aloud till sunrise. Harold got so into it he leapt about and recited with such gusto the young woman in the room above banged the floor with her shoe. Neither Harold nor Shakespeare would say they thought it was a stiletto, though it was.

*

Cowbells. Listen. Harbingers. Mapping their path to torment and death. Out of the night they come.

Symphony No. 8

DON'T YOU FIND it noisy? I mean, all those voices taking up the space?

No, not at all, he said. A thousand voices to replace a thousand I have lost from my head. I find them reassuring—agreeing and communing with each other, making a consensus of being.

*

Harold had wanted to be an astronomer. Harold *was* an astronomer, but not in an officially recognised way. Fuck the state. I don't want their certification, he said to Lucida—to *her*—as they stared at the stars from a blanket on a beach near Geraldton. *Her* said, You're such a conceited bastard, *Hal* (she emphasised the 'Hal'). *Her* said, Just shut up and looking at the damn stars and enjoy your insignificance. I can hear them, he said, And they are saying nothing about anything or anyone being insignificant. People go on about some of them being dead before they arrive here, but most of them are still alive, I can assure you. They are indifferent to our thanatos. He feared *her* would break into lines from the shitty play she was preparing for, but she didn't. She just nudged away from him a little, making a dip in the sand beneath the blanket beneath them both, which he slightly rolled into like into the hollow of a wave but pulled himself back out fast to ride the crest and fall over to the other side and undo the harmonics the waveset. He ID'ed a bunch of stars and kept their names to himself because he'd renamed them all, or thought of their Yamaji names which made a lot more sense to him. My head is an astrolabe he said, and she said, You sure know how to ruin an occasion. But he knew she was thinking other things, other powerful things that had nothing to do with him. He was just there, nothing more. He wasn't even an accoutrement, which both he & she knew would be an easy and unjust insult, a deployment of thought-words not even worthy of the unworthy moment. A seagull played the star's reflection off the sea. No clouds. No moon. The moon was such a rare visitor in Harold's reminiscences. Ghost crabs were moving up from the sea, some were already digging, digging near them, beneath them, but they and the blanket were already gone, wandering through the interdune corridor, past the rigorous salt-hardy plants, the plants making do without fresh water, up to a borrowed vehicle—someone's guilt-attempt to keep them together, even though they wanted them apart for good, forever. Divided paths. Head as an astrolabe, Harold tall and gangly and already fading in fertility, looked up and ate starlight. He ate knowing 'the speed of light' was the propaganda hook capitalist progress had caught itself on, *her* father an investor in such empiricism, such science of greed. Listen, listen, seabreeze, land cooling fast, two swing around fast. Music of the spheres. Moonrock. Skylab. Tektites. Cults with deathrays-in-development. This state-of-being that thinks it created him out of its anxiety, its prophecies, its mediums in orange and lilac and powder-blue lace-shawled lamps with batik prints on walls and indeterminate but massively present music as if all small stereos are on at once and lifting whole beachside suburbs to transportation, to crystals and hand-struck jewellery, kilns and artsy flair. Massive. Together lifting the world off its feet, willing it all on and on—results, outcomes, fulfillings. But sometimes the red & the black: the rooms suggesting blood and a starless night. The interior of planets. The crush of the core. Fingernails and scratch marks on the back. Installations of fear—the heart with the pin in it, the motorcycle skull-face-mask draped over the room divide, ready to pick up on the way out. Those trips she wanted to open the door into the next level of acting, of becoming. Conduit.

*

But really, what Harold remembered when telling Shakespeare wasn't the kicking by the neo-Nazis, but the fact that fellow protesters (he was one, but by osmosis) questioned his right to understand the consequences of Brexit because he wasn't really British. They said they could tell by his accent, which all admitted was really an indeterminate slur, but with something 'Australian' behind it. You cannot appreciate what it feels like to be English when other

English are racists, they said. You are not feeling our pain and our shame and our anger, because you can't. Doesn't compute, does it, said Shakespeare. I fear, said Harold.

*

You always talk in generics.

I am trying to be respectful—I feel there are things I should say, should pretend I know, hold sway over.

Do you know who I am?

You are a person. You live in Royston. You work somewhere in Cambridge. You commute by train. Only on some, not all trains that go between London and Cambridge stop in Royston. I have been to Royston, and have passed through the bus terminal—or bus changing point—many times.

Would you describe me as British?

If you want to be British, I am happy for you to be that. I am no believer in nation or states.

My father was born in the Punjab, my mother in a small village in a disputed region of Kashmir. Her father was an English businessman.

Okay.

You see, that trajectory, those variables of ethnicity and identity are important to my understanding of my Britishness. They make it a different Britishness . . .

. . . from?

Other Britishnesses. Yours is also an imperial-affected or inflected Britishness.

I am not British. I am nothing. And all Britishness is

imperialism. To join the club, is to join the club, in whatever capacity.

See, you are judgemental. You cannot know.

I cannot. And I don't.

I visited the Punjab for the first time in my life only last year. It was a revelation. The planets, the stars not only looking different from there, they are. Here, look at this from the Punjabi Tourist commission . . . wait, let me scroll down:

WELCOME TO NEHRU PLANETARIUM (LUDHIANA)

Run by Municipal Corporation, Ludhiana, Nehru Planetarium situated next to Rose Garden, Ludhiana play shows on solar system, moon, stars and other astronomical objects.

Timings

Monday to Thursday: 10:15 AM and 11:15 AM

Sunday: 3:15 PM, 4:15 PM and 5:15 PM

Closed on Fridays and Saturdays and Gazetted Holidays

Tickets General Public: Rs. 5

Student and Children below 10: Free
Contact: 0161-2771447

I went on my own because my sister wasn't interested. But I was. I went at 10.30 A.M. on a Tuesday. The show played and I realised they were different stars and even the earth's moon was different. As my Britishness is different from yours. What I possess is different.

I celebrate your difference, I respect it, but I am not British. I don't like mobile phones.

You are very alone. Without community you are lost.

Communities that are part of larger communities that manufacture and use and sell arms are communities lost.

I hear your ex- is the movie star . . .

Please don't mention her name. She is nothing to do with me. I am nothing to do with her.

You are a very lonely and bitter old man.

I am not that old, really.

*

Really, I saw your spirit leave your body and fly out over the fens, said The Stalker. THE STALKER!

It left me long ago, in the wheatbelt bushland. And then the bloke on the block up the road sailed in with his front-end loader and cleared all the bush away around the brook, the only water source that hung in there most of the year. He absolutely went for the throats of the flooded gums, attacking their gnarled bolls with fury, driving the night-birds away in broad daylight, their young devastated, bladed over into the dirt he revealed to the blistering sun. Then my spirit left me. Then the true stereotype found wings of death and sneered back in his mirrors, but he saw nothing but the emptiness he'd hoped to create. But that emptiness was full, and that emptiness was a bird that came from me but didn't belong to me; I was just a branch for it to settle on temporarily, disturbed from its spot. So you tell an untruth—if a spirit left me, it was not the one that chose me, not my 'own' . . . it was something else, if anything at all. The stereotypes of the Australian bush are not acts of violence because they are the norm, they are what that Euroconcept is built out of like the first movie theatre. Pathfinder. Pathogen. The body that doesn't desire your body or any other body a dead thing that has been vacated or must be vacated asap. What you saw was your own drone tracking me breaking free of its commands. What you saw was the liberty to watch, to mine the materials to make flight, to make spirit. An attack.

I was in Paris recently and saw The Woman with the Child in the Musée Rodin. She is single again now, did you know. She was looking at a bust of Mahler. You know, the effort and care of his and Alma's Paris sojourn post New York (& the big stuff). Rodin scribbled on the neck. Looking over the girl's head, I could see this clearly. But neither mother nor daughter knew I was there—I was incognito. Though mother sniffed the air, as if she recognised a familiar or slightly disturbing scent. I *am* self-aware.

I am not interested in Rodin's bust of Mahler. I am only interested in his music, and listening in my own company.

Yes, I've noticed how agoraphobic you're becoming.

Leave them alone.

And they'll come home?

Please, stop pestering me. Leave me in peace!

*

You will come to the forest? You will lock on? You will help us help the forest—the last bit of ancient woodlands in the region? The Woman and Her Child will be there. She has had a difficult time. She is homeschooling the child now—the child is excelling though the woman is growing weary. And I, Sab Woman, will watch over us all. But we feel we need you there.

As a mascot? A symbol of god knows what?

There's so little left of you, I doubt we can claim mascot status for you. No, just you. Because I know you know about these things.

Because you plan to expose my past and draw attention, to draw *her* to the protest, to make it flash around the world.

She is so famous, Harold. So very famous and potent.

So potent?

Yes. Her face is ubiquitous. And now that ancient photograph of you both as little more than teenagers lodged in those hills, between the rocks surrounded by *jay* trees . . .

You mean jarrah trees. Perth Hills. 1985.

Yes, that image of you fighting tooth and nail against the land developers.

She was pissed off with her old man at the time, but mostly doted on him. He loved the mines up north, and he loved his property portfolio down south.

Well, if we could set you up here and get an image and

juxtapose it and show it was *you* . . .

Well, you're blunt and ruthless . . .

No, choice, Harold. We're in the endgame.

Heilige Anachoreten gebirgauf verteilt, gelagert zwischen Klüten.

*

A survivor from an American shooting massacre will be coming to speak to the group. Please, can you be there. Will you read a poem?

I don't read my poems anymore.

I heard you read in Cambridge a few months ago. It was moving.

I regret it. I shouldn't have read.

I will never forget it.

I have forgotten it.

This isn't something to be glib about. Please?

I don't know. I am a ghost.

People are dying. The planet is being killed. You can speak for it.

I can't speak for anything, not even myself.

We don't care about your self, per se.

Now, I can make sense of that. You're saying something worth listening to. I will think about it.

Where are you living?

I am sleeping on Shakespeare's couch.

Where, in Stratford?

No, in Cambridge. I am walking back there today.

From here? From the Tate Modern?

Yes. I am not going inside. I haven't been inside for a year.

Walk all the way to Cambridge like Syd Barrett.

Not like Syd Barrett. But like thousands and thousands of others over centuries.

But we are locked in by the M25.

I pretend it's not there.

Dangerous.

It's all dangerous, it's all bloody.

A lot of planes overhead.

A lot. I have been asked to go to an ancient woodland.

It's the same meet. It's the same occasion. It's a line in the sand, so to speak. We are all gathering there and emanating outwards.

I have time for the Quakers. There'll be Quakers? I am not luring her there. I won't be part of that.

Who is *her*? I think we're speaking at cross purposes. One end, maybe, but many approaches.

*

Harold, the landlord has *commented*—he thinks you're creeping back in through the front door with a key from me. Which is true. He's not happy. But don't worry, I feel suddenly happy to have you here. Actually, if you want, we can collect your phonograph or cd player or music machine or whatever it is from the house in the field on the edge of the woods, and you can play your Mahler when I am out. Quietly.

That's generous of you, Shakespeare. I have to say, it's disturbing to experience such generosity. I will be bolder going to the bathroom now—I've been careful, avoiding the others who never liked or knew me anyway.

You're wrong there—it was really only me who ever complained about you. The others just thought you should wash more often and worried you didn't eat.

Okay. Thanks. I have decided not to join the protest, to hear the speeches.

Funny, I was thinking of getting over there myself. I never do these things. I never say anything—I think it, but then fall back into research. I satisfy myself that I edge towards contemporary truths my critiquing the past. But maybe the time has come. Critical. Point of no return.

They are trying to use me to lure someone else in to boost their social profile.

If it's for a worthy end, does it matter? You said to me a couple of weeks ago that you were the walking dead—what's it matter to you if you're hurt by something from your past. How do you think it makes me feel knowing I have a corpse on the couch who calls out to me at three in the morning and asks if I still get erections? Well, that's my business, and I don't really know that you don't!

I sometimes think the reason the world is vanishing around us is because we haven't fixed it in adequate description. That desk you work on, under a window that remains open even at night so your fluorescent desk lamp light merges with streetlight, so people walking past came look up into your illuminated face, the play of pane and eyeglass and text and skeletons of defoliated bushes then budding then leafing over your thoughts. And those books piled askew, always ready to fall, and the computer laptop pushed to the side in favour of notebook and pen, and the pair of dirty socks that sit next to your never washed and constantly rebooted coffee cup. The salt and pepper hair that is whiter than pepper, the tiny photo in a one-pound-shop frame far too large for it and all flaking silvered plastic of someone who means a lot to you but you won't say. Maybe a *daughter*? She is young but her face is so covered by her coat, snow around. And now I am wondering because of my eschewing of describing or absorbing description if it's not the child, the difficult and brilliant and terrifying child of The Woman. Are you why she is in Cambridge? Is it you that kept her from making more than a couple of visits to me in the basement? The curtains will fall into place when you change to sleep but never completely cover the contents of this room—large for the house, large enough to have your tiny kitchenette and a couch and your desk and a table and chairs and two cupboards of twisted plywood and false mahogany, varnish sealing the exposed floorboards. I heard every creak from the basement, every exposure of foot to floor. You in your socks, shoes by the door—a single pair of boots that no longer polish. But you let me wear my sandshoes even onto the couch because they are welded to my long, thin bony feet. See, I am more self-aware than you think. See, a poem was never a description for me—for all the details of where I was I included, for all the observations. It was different. It wasn't description for mood or setting, or even description for its own sake. For the joy of recording. I have lost that anyway, along with my erections. But maybe it's better that way.

As you don't follow the news you won't have heard

there's been another mass shooting in America. A school. An ex-student. An A15. Army reserve training. And a statement from a police representative that it saddens him that the memory of school the children who survived will carry with them through life is of the shooting. In the gore of weapons, in the blitz of the amendment, this is the way words form in all sincerity in gun-smoke air hungry for speech bubbles.

It's why I stopped listening to Nine Inch Nails. *Downward Spiral* plays in heads that can't process it. But it's not a cause, but a reflection of a disturbed machine that kills itself. Flesh is to be transformed into capital, shares, the invocations of the NRA. I will go to the protest, I will hear the speeches, I will see if she comes. She might not.

And that's what will finish you once and for all? Truth be had?

Yes. Yes. Yes.

*

There were well over a thousand people at the site. He stood where they wanted him to stand, he let them push the hair off his face, they photographed him next to an ancient oak. They released the image to all social medias with the caption: Australian Poet Harold X, long-term resident of Cambridge and the fens, once partner of the famous actor Lucida, has travelled over to the protest site to lock onto this magnificent tree. He says, if it dies he will die. And variations on this to fit the needs of the platform. The message reached Lucida in Hollywood instantly—she never slept and she watched feeds on HERSELF constantly. She was shocked and furious. He had NEVER done anything like this. He had politely vanished and rotted away. And now he was exploiting her. She phoned and woke her agent. She spoke to her lawyer. She ignored their advice and said, Get me on a flight to Heathrow ASAP!

*

She carried a small folder of his poems with her. She had destroyed photos, official documents of their relationship, even of their deceased child. But she still had a dozen of his poems dedicated to her. Taking a drink and nodding to the flight attendant who slipped quietly out of her first-class cabin, she read:

Once I Was Called Gretchen

The sun drives me underground—
I cannot read by its light. I pray for night.
I shed my skin for you every time I wake,
and the roots that have drawn me down
remake a canopy, a crown. An aura
of foliage I can't claim, but grows
out of me. Where else can I go?
What is lost will regrow.
The lights of the stage remain.

It annoyed her, it had always annoyed her. You are talking about you, not me, she said. There's no light of redemption for either of us. Just loss. You besmirch even the restitution.

But their life together was already finished and she spoke to thin air. She would make the public her children. She would be potent. Hal could go to hell, as far as she was concerned. And she had had so many lovers, so many better lovers since. And she heard him laugh-cry back, Who cares about lovers? I detest that word. A commodification, Lucy, a commodification. Don't call me that, only my father calls me that. I'd rather be called *she* or *it* or *her*, thank you. I delete you from my life. You've held me back long enough. And it was done. And so was Western Australia. And then Australia. For all the claims the country still made on her, for all the tourist campaigns they based around her, for all the bridges she made for the philistines searching for ways into the fascist towers of the newest America. She was one of the possessors of the key. She hadn't aged. Harold looked absolutely awful. She could never respect someone who'd let himself go to the dogs. Hideous.

*

Three unities. That's why. And I don't believe, not even slightly.

*

It's easy to be shallow, but an artform to convince yourself that such shallowness is purposeful, necessary and adequate. So said Shakespeare to Harold, who was getting antsy and wanting to leave. He had heard she was coming. It was all the talk. But he didn't want to be there.

The cameras will follow her here whether I am around or not. I accept that I've been used—you know, for a good cause. I am okay with that. Now I want to go. Her shallowness will drown me, and drown us all. You have no idea how deep it goes with her, this performance of supreme vanity and unconcern with anything that doesn't serve 'her'. She is not who you think she is.

'Hoy-day, what a sweep of vanity comes this way!'

Precisely. You have no idea! And the reality: she is soulwise without vanity!

*

Harold had many tics as a child and it took him decades to shake them. Now his shuffling absorbed all tics, ironing them out into a 'traffic hazard'. The prejudice he received just took on a different mask. I have tried to iron myself as a patch onto their collective identity, but failed. His grandfather had a 'gammy leg'—Harold's father (did he remember him?) said, It's the *de rigueur* war wound, take no notice Harry. Harold's mother said, The poor man has suffered—he detests war and war is always with him. Harold's father (was it him?) gave him a clip under the ear for imitating his grandfather's twitchy leg. Don't be daft, son, there's nothing wrong with your leg! Sometimes Harold stood on one leg, but that was because he loved and imitated birds. He could stand under the Great Tree for hours watching birds of all sorts standing on one leg, keeping cool.

The Woman's daughter came up to him as he was standing on one leg in front of the oak, a chain nearby waiting to be looped around his body, and said, The ducks are worth saving—there are no ducks here but when all the trees go the ducks will eventually go, too.

You are right there, said Harold.

I am having some time off school. I don't like school, but I like going to school to play and be with my friends and I like it when we do plays.

You are a social being, said Harold. He wasn't experienced enough, say as a parent or guardian, not to add, I am not.

You don't like people?

No, not much.

I like people. But I don't like the world—it makes me angry.

I have seen you angry. You get very angry.

The girl smiled, stood on one leg imitating Harold, and said, I do. And as Mummy says, There's plenty to get angry about. Mummy says we might be going back to Australia, that it's not so prejudiced there. My school says it's not prejudiced but it is. It has little white lies and little white tricks. I can see them.

Australia is very prejudiced, said Harold. But Brexit makes it ring loud like bells here. But there are bells—there are loudmouths down there spouting white lies, too.

I will be angry with them as well, them, said the girl. Mummy says I have a brother in Australia who lives with his father. He's not my father but he is my brother. I should very much like to meet him.

You're full of surprises today. You don't need to stand on one leg. The police are coming now. I am going to chain myself to this tree. You go and find Mummy.

You're funny, Duck Man. You don't have a phone? I hate phones. Phones are tools of the little white liars, too.

You're sharp.

Mummy says the Famous Actress is on her way. Will she talk to me?

She'll probably only talk with you. Now scoot, before you get arrested.

Ha! I would like to get arrested. Silly old police. Silly. Silly. Silly!

*

Chorus Mysticus (discarded fragment):

I have never admired men—
they have set an agenda of destruction—
and the women who have followed the men
have reformed the pain without correction.

*

Hear ooze taste owl screech see echo of bumblebee. And all those introduced species, needing life, too. Wherever. So long without eating, the body breaking down to keep the sense alive to shifts across zones of habitation. The endemics. The invasions. The thefts. The seeking out of a foothold, of life. In the whirl of contradictions the baton, which falls in front of the cameras. Deny the senses is the only gateway out. Already dead. To the world. The bandicoot ears raised dead on the road. To reverse and confront. Not *your* doing, but a doing. All culpable. Tomorrow, if one left, you just as easily. Scavenged by crows which are hated. And here, as he is falling, against the great trunk, the gnarls and Greenman hopes, the ghost evocations and callings for what can't be right, if you're a victim of folklore. Fox hunt. In Beverley, Western Australia. In reds near here, there, where bones fold over, skin flaps under the coat. All the decay, all the biology preserved, all the peat that burns that wets that holds that smothers that grows in its own way. As salt does, spreading out from its eye, its scald. Lakes appearing outside the walkings. New as a meteorite strike. What are you going to do, sad in the stubble: like glass if you run through without shoes, or even with shoes, say puncturing flip-flops—thongs—like nails. Nailed in the paddock, the field. As authentic as ploughman's lunch, as twists of Latin and mediaeval French and foul papers and poet-soldier gentleman courtiers the women of the court secret speaking for what else can they do with the deliverance of flowery lines? Empire. You see, strontium atom. You see the building blocks of the falling buildings, the ponds with seagulls floating prim upright in accordance, the board the trust, the energy musts. It hasn't gone away the cradle to grave. Cycle. Pitfalls of waste. No, lights edging closer to remnant ancient wood to the forests of the southwest of where he comes from, the jarrah crowns dead without state funerals, root to ceiling, ceiling to root: all those cricket Manhattans travelling the shadowy empire of sports, the clinging clinging on to deadwood so tinder tender burn and estates the new houses as we all need somewhere to live, to live, the train station of Sellafield the windscale magnavox evaporation mox mox storage plutonium decommission stringing it out boring to hear just there get on with non-life take care seagull leakpond all those Irish authors such English literature such convict labour such starvation such willing away B30 and B38. And now, and now, the estate will be built and the estate with golf course and strand and empire invigorated anyone can play with members and investments of flesh, blood, DNA. Earthspeak we're always letting language invent replace such a life of its own referents shed to ghost a new greenhouse us and our surroundings and Pacific test islands where growback is plantsong to jolly up the toxifying of all you see such an inheritance under the glare of sun and planets and singsong chatty stars for we glare back even through an atmosphere thick as a brick.

Who are *The Boys* that chorus in her wake, she begging for my soul as if the deed were all about her? Maybe it is, filtered as she is. It pains, this recall. That's bitter, and only an echo coming back from earlier distress.

He thinks in his halfness. I was a young angel, a chorister, he muttered to the window as he walked out without breaking the glass. I sang against the tide against the voices and was forced out. The bitterness is in the soaring collapse, the flight over forest now gone, the desert that's now left even to be desert. Those anchorite mining camps of porn and amphetamines, and that was then as now, the underpinning I . . . we . . . needed to compose against, rush from. I could not boy the girl voice into safety, my traits belonging nowhere. The crack came late but I was already out of the set. These ordered thoughts, this holding the note beyond tolerances. I hear it, but they never did. Can't. We were all called 'innocent', but it didn't protect us from the excoriation of our surroundings, our habitat.

Did Harold tune this to his failed New World ambitions, stuck in the moist coiling cold of the stony town in the fens? He had wanted to hear to experience the orchestra and chorus of a thousand, of thousands, even, in the glittering glass city of spikes, in the New Amsterdam, but this dream fell as *her* actuality rose.

Flower meltdown in forest deletion like rogue wave holes, rogue holes in sea which species will be let to hang on not I not I. Freak waves that take out the tallest lighthouse lanterns.

But it wasn't as concrete as that as the aspirational; this blossoming crowd sourced crowd funded downfall crowing as the rookery is dismantled the splintered broken-free gravity voices.

CHORUS MYSTICUS [american typewriter]

Corrective election
a picnic spread
artificial selection
wined and dined
perfecting intention
to increase spiritual profit
extinction rebellion ignores vegan effort
and devices proliferate.

Harold heard the anachronism with its consumer hope and clamouring seep in a bit, heard a bit seep in, but stood looking at the swan standing up on the water making anti-prayer of its wings to stay precise as the moment he'd be perfectly lost in. This, he thought, is the consequence of the drop of blood spilt in our initial love-making, those decades ago so present now, in the end. *Schöpfung durch Eros. Hymne.* Where is the offspring of our gathering, our union? I hymn to no one but the woman with the difficult child. That woman heard me and listened and then was gone once her child descended from the tangled tree of life and rejoined the flow of their lives which weren't and aren't mine, in which and of which I have no part. This old codger shuffling along—a fox terrified by the galloping, the blast of the nasty horns of triumph. But then so many voices, children's voices of delight out of which he could pick the difficult child's enthusiasm, off-key energy, and he thought, She is a visionary but no one will see it other than her mother. And me, Harold, alone. I wish her well, I pray for her protection and deliverance, for an eventual epiphany that will draw her back to mother upon whom she will inevitably turn her back in order to shine before her peers, make herself soar above herself, so fraught with climbing and being spiky against the pastoral.

I have no solo, no voice to lift, and yet, alone. What other way? This town is an alone town, against all the clustering, the May days and balls, the social exercising. Here, you can be so alone. So on the greens, vulnerable to resentment, selected and abandoned. Here, in this learning, this greenery and stoniness. Alone passing alone, shuffling.

Symphony No. 9

ALL BITS AND pieces all tubes and whiteness i detest whiteness the blanking the pseudo neutrality when so much is invested by THEM in the glare, to be wheeled by bully-beef intern who smiles because he has to smile in his greens as if he & i share gender when i am no gender never was and sexless as anaesthetic which now she hovers over me and outlines the cold tubing and says it will just be a little prick and then you'll forget keep talking keep alive in death because now you want to speak endlessly who was that critic who spoke of 'vocabular music' that was it of high & low that was style and that was an inflection of homelessness & she said i will be there she will be there when i come out when i am pasted back together the damaged the crushed the torn all sewn into a shape vaguely resembling me and i an australian an unbritish an un any nation these weapons of culture the brit invasion the attack guitars the swinging london the freedom no one had in trident sailing the seven seas or not quite seven a league a league a league but barely twa corbies the procedure the money she'd been putting into that account for decades that account that segues into barclays the slave bank the cane bank the sugar pot the trove the black & white minstrel show the listening listening to make rip-off art the collection at king's the british museum logos protectorate basement prices and movie set seriously she's shot four films in there *in thar* under pillars by ledges and pigeon laments one way or another and in the spiralling guggenheim where she met trent though who's to say what went on creatively just coming within vicinity a sleeper a knockout never shuts down dna still bubbling who wants the ancestry revealed the kit that says a bit of this and a bit of that so you can suddenly lay claim to an entire people's suffering as if you will always part of it to disown as soon as needs be? who is she, really? needle in the hay. hay monet stacks. lozenges in paddocks those stacks we make those forms we take those seas we cross that ms liberty at the opening of a liberty of arms sales it all comes back it all does it all awakes.

all there all there to see me to hear me and see me and deport me. shakespeare says always hamlet always back there always country always place i have none of and that wants none of me in my brief stay in vienna uncouth after crossing australia with her crossing in the mid 80s and on the plains and bluebush delusion of presence and whales and humpbacks in the bite and the bustard always back with her and then to vienna and then the pregnancy and the opera house and she had a voice she tried out but show pony show pony almost swept up and blown away by massive truck on the eyre on the wiley on the trek across where not to go no land of ours from west to east and yet every step a stealing step even where no water allowed tribes to be but they knew and beneath in the caves thylacines were more than bones and ghosts were truths that walked with sinew and gristle and we knew and shared and i loved her embodied and i was fertile on the karst and we knew we knew and sang silent too because we had no rights east to west and her father was a shadow we ignored in the sunlight though clouds came over and drizzled and emu families on edges on plains on test on take on toxicity on take back after we've tested our testaments and made language fit and given words to oxford to the lexicon of presence more than way way to skin a world a country a zone and cold war predilections. all of that was then i abandoned. don't leave the house without don't leave whitewash don't leave house without arbiter and drip and he's here a friend late and she and the woman and sab and 'the undiscovered country from whose bourn no traveller returns' is all of them homeless on an island they define as aircraft carrier as if it were a moment that echoes through time & space and all people are welcome to the show to follow the single thread the sound of sticks the sound of wind the sound of a flute leading you astray in emergence.

*

in the forest into the forest from the paddock into the forest because death tells us so tells us that's where we go to die as colonials but then we colonials bulldoze it away and there's nowhere for us to wander to be cast to wrestle with dappled light unless it's through the metal leaves of skyscraper foyers or in the piazzas that welcome us to the passing gestures of postmodernism those trees death tells us so will go and salt will come to corrode the evidence of our having been because death tells them so tells them to act while they can and wipe us out because there are colonials and colonials and some are compositors of wealth and power and they will snuff the lesser colonials as they and the lesser colonials have snuffed the custodian-owners letting back only as long as it serves them acknowledging so business can get done allowing performance because their own wealth can elegantly accrue with baubles of conscience.

drums open the door to listening to our departure our entry to whatever niche death accords the entertained the lavished upon—the summer gone and back to work and back to work the summer gone the shadows of our allotments of time/timing—this result this hangover from 1907 when harold's grandfather was lambasted by the school authorities for expressing sympathy with the zulus and compounding it by saying he thought the empire was wrong this child with audacity with words beyond his years with wickedness in his heart was caned with a brutality that made him sing out made him sing like a machine like a mishap at the sunshine harvester works like a decision to go elsewhere to return on the slow boat to fremantle to go back to the wheat the harvester chewed up—his unionist father saying to him, 'they will always hate what they don't understand they will flash like the gunpowder that has got them where they are'—enigmatic persecuted but lining up to war against war to be shot down holding to account the a contradictions of his own trajectory—this breaking down of listening to death—a ripple across the river an osprey piercing the surface a caspian turn red billed and watching intently along the device the mechanism—remember back remember back the vast attacks remember back the little brazen trumpets in the gallery remember back—as vast as the arid zone as vast as the trumpets blasting incendiary total deletion erase of air the blasts the test the testing times the aftermath of aftermath.

*

we can't stick to the shape the movements. you overlay, like *dark side of the moon* & wizard & oz. you've been given the formula in prior collapsed curves, rainbows with more colours than you can see though it's all emperor's new clothes (as said, as said before). implore, each biography of each player. each difficulty getting to the stage, the crises that follow later. that letter it mattered that letter with all the cambridge and some london and even some australian poets—and two visiting americans and also three nigerian poets and two from israel and two from palestine—all saying what you have done matters those two chapbooks those journal poems those poems some of us were lucky to hear you read recently . . . those new poems those poems that are part of a writing that has not stopped . . . those poems all brought together are a 'substantial body of work' that we'd like to see published in a single volume and we'd publish it by subscription and bring it out for those interested to not only read but talk and yes argue, argue a lot probably over, over it all. that letter it mattered he had to confess. i confess i say it gives me something to footnote as purpose, the vanity of it, i know i regret but yes, it has mattered to me. i should keep quite i know, i write to her i write to land i write to ghost. i wrote. i was? what immigrant i always am and why no one wants this immigrant? i welcome refugees where it's not my right to welcome but i do and i opened my basement and the house—a small small house—in the field—to those who'd come overland but said nothing of this because to reveal is to be booted out one's self and maybe i should but where to go i have nowhere but the text in my head not even the pages now not that i'd burn them but just leave them to the damp the mildew the river that ate erasmus's bones. i read biography and listened to vinyl and the tooth in the groove and hoped for insight to incite my passion to make lines but they wavered and the mildew *the mildew* and yes to realise to realise that isolde was present was over the shoulder was the swim in the lake the hike in the mountains was exercise and rhythmic exchange as total conducting and that's what drove the symphonies that's what drove the need to take the baton into the score and run riot run from riot to move on from persecution.

*

you see it comes back to me it comesback the pillbox hat the pillbox burner in the backgarden the burning out the carpet bombing the flamethrower the camouflage stuck into the helmet net island hopping the dug in dug out the filmography even something like the man in the grey flannel suit we watched together and I had pain of memory of warplay and she said i could play betsy though you're not greg peck and i said pillbox hat i wasn't boy enough to play with many of the boys and the girls rejected me as an effeminate boy though i had no interest in any of their games and toys and favoured neither blue nor pink the era still matters because we are product of and not just history to faux liberations as the planet heaves and speaks its gasping last words which just leads to critical theory of machine gun nests and culpability all those little desires i locked away in scientific investigations i suppose i saw myself as alchemist though turned gold into nothingess the analogues of life.

*

there is a poet a poet who knew about the generics of forests a truth of biosphere more than specificity though journeys in europe made him see all wrong when he thought he saw light and darkness clearer his name was brennan, my friend shakespeare, and for all his effusion he saw clearly and knew what centaurs might do and undives out of water to fluidics of presence as we all kneel to take a drink without cisterns of empire to declare a civilised control we lack through that but in brennan we see the mallarméan faun set free because he was freer in the trees of an antipodes he didn't quite see as plundered in his church vestments as child of the father and students of the father and abandonment to return all the rituals he relied on not to see & smell the eucalypts left from rapine and murder and theft and thought he crossed the seas for roots of languages he curled through prayer and administration of souls he uttered: 'The forest hides its horrors, as the sea' such translation loss as 'House of Pan' and yet how much could he see of language in soil and leaves and trails passing under and through whose people the people whose knowledge as vast as all the poems and music and control mechanisms of prayer he called upon? this links me to all the manifestations of self the obsession the monstrous ego lurchings and leaning and yearnings and plunging into a smooth fork of york gum and complex easy song of mistletoe bird i don't have to see to be with unobtrusively for that's the key to me not spying but seeing and what valéry built on saying master but meaning only his madness for vision, too, a shared communal thing really a sharing and saying coming in despite all the silences in zones while shifting around we can all come in given codes but don't have to, shakespeare, all those horns the chase the Sab woman i couldn't share a bed with but she is good and decent and gives her time to more than pleasure though she gains pleasure from seeing justice and to think marx was in london for so long with family and observed and factored in but still empire wouldn't crack under the strains of abused workers and the canons would be manned and womaned and the royals still called them to the streets to watch on and but the cups with jewels stencilled on with whatever tech the boffins could come at a given time the pride the british ingenuity the bulldog's savaging of kicked up cancan heels.

Symphony No. 10

DR WHO ONLY likes *the magic flute* walk with me walk with me for walking makes its own music even with my odd gait my different way of stepping out i was never a model dancer though she wished i were talented in her own right architect of my prosody who only likes the magic flute and for whom other music musis as a whole is meaningless but who extracts all going forward from the one-way street the notes as cliffhangers the analysis of such a bursting collapsing ego;

she says that her parents never argued because father would never allow arguments but mine argued till he was gone and mother loved grandfather—her father-in-law—more than father loved his own father with the gammy leg always carrying on about war and the government sucking everything out of it they could forever to make themselves strong; i went out of the house with shouts in my ears and heard a trumpet playing somewhere that was in the suburb on the edge of the bush and the river before we went away and i followed the thin but sharp line of the trumpet and i hummed along and then the row broke out of the house and the birds in the lines fell from the sky and the song in my head became jagged but i reassembled it and remembered it watching antlions kick sand from the eye of their pits to make them more deadly and the trumpet line was lost to someone else's life alone;

she says that i was obsessed with an 'eternal feminine' and that i do 'she' the 'he', i am stuck and i make mystery where there's no more mystery but then i say i ghost and i am not and never was and that's a wrong interpretation but i will say sorry anyway sorry as i should because i was and wanted to be even if i said otherwise and what role have those around me given in my narrative of denial and oblation that wasn't really an offering to anything more than the self this cypher world i have inhabited across decades of narratives that avoid the elephant in the room because i saw an elephant once made of metal a mosaic of different coloured metal being hauled up toodyay road toward dowerin maybe but anywhere really a giant elephant on a trailer passing the roadside clearing the felling of big tree roosts nesting places and marri blossom out so you can tell the time of year though here surrounded by you all in the damp place with so much less rain in the fens which is low and holds holds holds the soakthrough but not the downpours as in other parts of the island that's a mistake outsider's make and i've been here hiding in public because that's what this place has become all people in one place whose eject and reject button doesn't totally work though some in uniforms and in rooms in rooms in rooms would have it so, so i say sorry Sab Person and Sorry Parent Person and Sorry Shakespeare Person and sorry Actor Person and Sorry Parent People and truly sorry to those whose land i usurped in making poems of unbelonging having nowhere else to turn i should have remained completely silent garrulous at this end crushed by The Stalker by the constabulary the state the university the arms industry the weaponry of building of music companies of music administration of the cd industry of microsoft of facebook on instagram of apple of ibm of the long list of inserts into the chain into the cyborg we put cart before horse to make rights so we can exploit i am not part of old man not that old really though an end is old isn't even even if i'd passed as young as ours did, ours, you never recover never pick up the pieces such loss and that's what we share and i know you hold me because of this and every role you've had is a mask to hold back your incredible sand anger your depths that will sweep over us all like the passing of the sun;

in the summer house on the paths between lakes and wetlands good order decomposes as poppies in lapels;

how we met we met not long after school (ignore what you hear of her fancy education . . . i was there and i can't keep feeding that myth) but different schools at a protest yes she protested then and was passionate and furious and even forget herself but the use of 'even' is unfair because all acting was a separate thread and she didn't make the act of protest theatrical she worshipped her father she complied and hated behind the scenes she was angry and kicked against the pricks and entangled herself with me and the lines i strung out not as snares because i didn't want to trap and hurt anything but lines to distract divert offer alternative paths not for noble reasons but because i wasn't sure of anything and images of violence spread like acne over my soul and i pushed them back dried them out made drought to revivify in search of moisture caught up in genderlessness and still performing as if i was part of, that's the gap the crevice that's the consultation in walks on walks;

and so the only music i hear and wish to hear the only spheres generating are ragtime tunes my mother played and interpretation that left her exhausted and knowing her limitations are appropriated pounding bass lines on stereos in enclaves of soldier-worship that says the army makes an even killing field the brass band that irritates the suffering in dormitory suburbs but not the flag-flying neighbours the neighbours with their union jacks the neighbours with their royal memorabilia as chants and cries of anger drinks break white audiences hooking their skis to broadening experiences in the spoken word confrontation with the lies of Euro-art we [we?] peddle to accomplices looking for a white translator to guide them through the theft—listen. listen. hear. hear? those desert songs we find a way to hear, the adapting routes to recording to broadcast to become one with. never forget the racist mahler as he experienced racism. never forget his statements in new york a little later a little after the sketching out but with the idea of new york of fidelio of toscanini rivalry embedded—these loose ends around the liminal pond, the crossing before or after, zweig playing chess on another boat at another time, the interpretations of the second viennese school the loving remake so many years later, and adding to the repertoire. never forget that his music couldn't absorb, that he himself added the constraints, the strait jacket, though the music itself tried to smash its way out of his cultural lockdown. a contradiction. a paradox. a tautology. listen, hear, the music of the spheres is necessity drives. survival and celebration in the face of assaults that keep coming but adapting. the borgness of whiteness the silver screen colourcoding the limitations the self-protection as all 'great men' ladle out the hypocrisies we let go to the footnote, the limelight as noisy as a tuning up in any parlance.

have a cuppa have a cuppa have a cuppa of green tea they say she they say you are so young at heart so vibrant and those few words, 'surely they can leave the little bits of ancient woodland left alone' have done more more than we imagined diminishing and expanding and infuriating yet giving hope giving hope so trapped we all are in this world of your making your guilt with frills;

we went to new york and i was to read and i read hart crane's *the bridge* instead and none of mine not a line and they said you have killed yourself off and she said, you did the best thing and you see i loved her for this and we discussed earthworms emanating out from central park emanating out under the luxury apartments one of which she owns now and spends a few weeks in each year when in town and why do i know this i who keep my head down and talk to the Sab woman through the night from my cot to her on the floor and swap lines with shakespeare only true true friend who most wanted me out of his orbit: 'We make guilty of our disasters the sun, the moon, and stars, as if we were villains on necessity, fools by heavenly compulsion': as if to trek with astrolabe that calenture we've walked towards north star guidance system the silos full of offerings we will take whether we like it or not like the fallout like the dispersal of soul materials materialism of presence this absolute doing their getting their job done . . .

*

. . . this is an end of exploration this is an end. This is an end. An end of Xploration. Of exploitation. Of poise and taste and dictation. Of repetition. Of lives delivered on a platter where few meals are taken. None can finish what is finished and unfinishable. Fish in the basement. Winter creeks. Dying river systems. Drained water sports festival drain. This is an end of exploration this end is the end. No amount of accelerant no amount of kindling. All those flames tapped outside car windows all those sparks that take away the archives all those burnings out. This exploration this self-gain this pathos this wreck of creation parsing crevices in deserts. And so in temples of learning as innocent as oak forests fallen to sail to jarrah the streets the wartime streets all records and schemes and settlements. Advisory boards to everything to all facets of miners of extraction industries of the atom split over drinks the coffee machine all of those texts wavering in exploration this end this end finished unfinished finito as we as he as they all said in childhood of a certain time and place like limericks memorised under duress to force a life's aversion. This is an end of exploration this is an end—know the grit the leaf, know the seed and how it transfers. O fini O singular O past O nominal O passive O passive O passive participle! To think to think they think I think the world began the world began 7,000 years a go at going a go at beginnings to think of origins and grammar. And that's where I trek across the 40,000 years of knowledge of presence of the land I was born into and forced into owning and then I read if 'You don't love it leave it' . . . and I did, but I love those whose land it is love with respect because of awe and a desire to learn what I have no right to learn so I left and went back and left and left and am nowhere. This churchlessness I inhabit this warding off this looking back to centre to sea that is emptied by the bulldozers—there, I declare my fear at this end of language for me this letting go of words, this discharge of data collected and fed and gathered and crumbed and desired yes desired I confess this lust for learning that has left me sterile in the eyes of many and redundant in my lack of synthesis and my poor comprehension in their way of measuring. What proof can I offer them when I don't wish to defend my lack of position, my irrelevancy on the fringe of town where I dwell and exist just exist and nothing much more with no claim that I should be more me in this self-obsessing. I understood nothing because I ate nothing I shared no dishes and was left outside looking at the foliage. A shallow, empty stomach, a senseless and insensitive person who stumbled from cultural realm to cultural realm. I did not want what was offered and yet I ate. I ate the herbs and the roots and grains. Sometimes I shared in that. But not in everything and the not in everything was louder than what was shared. So even full-stomached I was called empty. Not fitting in the eternal dining, the sharing that had an awkward place at the table I could not fill, ghost with foliage stomach. This is an end of exploration this is an end.

*

The stalker is here the stalker latching on to someone observed then to someone closer to the target. Always the aim was Lucida always the big-screen torment the goddess siren syndrome alive and well in inflections. She said, as she came for Harold, as he manifested in his final moments, as he appeared as a vulture over the soon-to-be-corpse of lingering DNA energy, as she came to him like a cloak of night like prayers in sunlight like the singularity he didn't even see Lucida standing by the bed watching the monitors without drama in her eyes alone with him but for the stalker who had her had her in a Mandible claw of almost empathy and in killing him softly he became part of a little of her that would also pass but no more quickly than anyone else at least two years of bodychemical adaptation to a new scenario a new stage in career not dissimilar to Picasso's Blue Period, not really but with twists of Arthur Boyd and Joy Hester in there, and artists who went to the core but not even Lucida herself would appropriate for the sake of the press to add another medal to the war chest to the inheritance of United Nations in the bliss of togetherness the market for equality that traded in futures and gave the one per cent all they needed to elevate to Elon Musk towards mass in heavylift, a battery of knowledge as spirit as the new archiving propelled outwards past the asteroid belt where it also might just might become as millions of bits millions of needles millions of crystals to melt in the boy's heart the boy in the backyard watching his half-sister burn it all out all of that *stalker-boy* watching from the picket fence watching what happens over and beyond and staying out long beyond coming in time the evening star Venus winking in a weird *uneasing* sort of way.

*

We all fall down we all cadence we all decay we all decadence decedents all fall all taxonomy all Romans earless in the scrub of vicissitude and now a smattering of snow is promised where seasons have gone away and cascade the case befalls us all, friend, friends, friends, in dust and red and endless nightlight scan of background chatter cadence of descendants old stone charters fall down all fall, friends, fiends all and not a trace of the rubato of youth not a trace? Untrue, unto, untoward. Here, let us read words you wrote when you were young and believed, when poems were the way through it all, to a truth to an action. Let us read, let us read to you with our collective ghost-breath, our sins wisping over the fens the rivers the oceans the mountains the snow drifts the wastelands the wasteland the dunes the hills the plains the dust the mineholes the waterholes the desire lines the paddocks mapped with a seeder's stretch of truth a header's harbinger theft of food bread basket heaped lies you wanted to annunciate outspeak what was left what could you do? From these bindings we read aloud read the ibis in the swamp the painting that haunts and lurks and lifts out of itself to tap stories it can't tap but we know the truth is bright and murky revealed and hidden and the era tracks through like certainty and the crimes of the past are eternally present as you wrote and wrote: We all fall down we all cadence we all decay we all decadence decedents all fall all—this all we make for ourselves then includes only those we can envisage whose eyes we think we know not all never all and not all fall or fell and that stand outside and beyond you and your masks stand far *far* away.

Earth Songs [Coda to The Mahler Erasures][4]

[4] It was supposed to be low-sky winter sunshine, but it wasn't. But then, not reading or seeing the icons or hearing mention of weather reports, he wasn't expecting it. His thumbs didn't prick anyway, though the red dawn suggested something was topsy-turvy. He was going to London, though he could ill-afford it. A day ticket. Where had the money come from?—he couldn't imagine unless she'd left it on his bedside table as a kind of tip for caring, for semi-tuning into her protest talk. For, truthfully, saying he didn't like the thought of a fox being ripped to pieces by dogs, or a dog with electrodes inserted into its brain, or some skincare treatment being ladled into its eyes. No great music can come of such things, he'd thought, if not said. He felt out of his usual register and wanted to break his patterns. He would go the Tate Modern and see what was on. He had no idea and had no desire to poke around in the usual places such information was stored. He thought, Shakespeare would know, but he was so distant of late, and so caught in a few lines of First Folio dubiousness, that he didn't want to ask. He would go, and listen to the visual arts, or the plastic arts or whatever. He knew he would be alienated, but he wanted to witness the turd on the toilet floor, laid down by a hater of modern art. There was always one in a male toilet somewhere in the building, maybe one left behind and one being laid down, at least during opening hours. Cleaners wouldn't soil their own work places.

Seeing a new town rise up between Cambridge and London, he thought of the state of the river, the valley. Somehow it flashed into his head that he would be distorted, would be mis-seen and would mis-see, that the colours of his situation would be exposed and he would be exposed to the same colours of others in their situations. He knew his solipsism would be revealed as narcissism in a group setting. That all his staring through windows at rain dripping down the panes and wondering at the maths of chaos segueing with the order of Mahler would expose a turgid beauty. The irony and agony of the earth's deathsong, which it didn't want to sing but was forced to rehearse and rehearse by the nanosecond. It was degrading.

Those concrete rooms. That big engine room hall. He could smell the carbon dioxide emanating, sense its making as he shuffled down the slope, gaining pace that almost tipped him over as the ground levelled out. And then he scraped entry, kowtowing, into the climate awareness studio of one hundred with private chef man's exhibition. He smelt the loss of moss in habitat, and muttering to himself, I wonder how many reindeer are going mossless for this immersive experience, a person next to him said, Shut up, you old philistine fool.

He shuffled on and looked through the lens and heard laughter through the wall. He was grabbed and pulled away, and a younger man was yelling at him, Come and experience with me, come now. He shuffled determinedly on with the younger man following and when he said, Please leave me alone, the man who popped a couple of triangular pills as he spoke, one sliding back out down his chin, said, Fair dinkum, mate, fair dinkum. And then the women stopped the younger man from following him into the fog tunnel, the ill-lit smog corridor where every lung ailment he'd ever had peaked in his chest and made sick rainbows and halos around him. He shuffled, and someone said, You look bloody frightening, mate. He wanted back to his basement and the 7th. The 7th on vinyl. The honesty of night and the owl he'd let roost in his head after its hunting. That was a different kind of hunt, wasn't it? It was. He shuffled into the financial district and shuffled on towards the British Library. He shuffled through puddles and vaping mist, he shuffled against heavy-handed crowds that almost knocked him over. He shuffled against cab horns and cyclists saying, You gotta a deathwish? He shuffled down lesser streets where the narrow dark sky walked to its guests with a familiar indifference. He shuffled against the history of Deutsche Grammophon. And by the time he got to Kings-X, it was in fact dark and beers were being handed out by way of a promo and he said, No, no, I don't want your green beer and the fog is already here and there's too much light at night. Cough. Yes, a new lung ailment brought on by . . . London, the fog? He'd wrapped himself in a London Fog coat for years, it had insulated him, but now it was gone. But he'd wrapped belongings in it . . . cds, hadn't he? A box set of cds. Yes, and pens and paper and a dog-eared . . . Lucida had once told him by the light of a Maralinga dawn—such dawns will always be with us now—she had told him, You're looking dogeared this morning. He coughed and the overhang of the station was suddenly dripping, and it was raining more heavily outside his head than inside. It washed the fog away.

He didn't accept that Cambridge was changing. Cambridge is not the university, he thought to himself, disturbed by the fields choked with animals for the vet sciences school. He found himself gently rubbing the nose of a horse and saying to it, I was inside a kaleidoscope of false lights and a tunnel of lying mirrors that let their maths rule their beauty, and now I am way off my line to sleep and with you here, and soon you will be bound with adamantine chains, soon the eagle will be picking at your liver. A winter owl flew through the night for it was dusk and he could see only the horse by the light of the full moon that had forced its way through the clouds. He found his way around by the dank smells and the feel, and with the rapid changes he grew disorientated and was nowhere. Nowhere is so easy and so corrosive, he thought. He found a bare tree—an oak . . . an oak he should have known, and curled up at its base though he was stricken by headlights . . . streams of cars that kept moving towards the M Road, indifferent to him . . . many of them heading to London, already burdened by too many routes, too many ways through to same places. Nowhere. The bicycle-tracked mud oozed nearby, a silt of once-fens-almost, of layers and layers to be pushed under new *knowledges*. He could hear fireworks but had buried his eyes in his cracked, cold hands. He could hear the kaleidoscope breaking through, the shower of sparks of election day. Someone's victory that wasn't one for anyone he knew—not for the horse, not for the tree. The bare tree hoping to sprout and make seasons till kingdom come's undoing.

It had taken Harold the best part of two decades to get away from Cambridge and make the return to Western Australia, but here he was again, still broke, back in Cambridge. He didn't have long to live—maybe six months—and he had chosen to spend that time in Cambridge, or in a suburb of Cambridge. Out past the Histon Road—not even his usual stomping ground. Just the best room he could find for the money, in a Cambridge that existed as if the students weren't part of it. That was his Cambridge, the Cambridge that went on even when the students weren't in residence in the colleges.

Harold had stopped listening to music, though Mahler's *The Song of the Earth*, his true ninth symphony, *Das Lied von der Erde*, kept throwing its pair of voices across his synapses. Two voice struggling with each other as reconfigured in his head. That old voice of love, sure, but also his anger with the brutality country was treated with where he came from. There was almost none of the old bush left, and what was left was being picked away at by the solo bulldozer as much as the phalanxes of corporate bulldozers. It was a deathzone.

In Cambridge again, he wandered or staggered along his old walking trails, knowing how extraneous he was, is. I am in the isness of my irrelevancy he said to his old friend, Shakespeare, who though he'd known a relatively short time felt like a long-term acquaintance. He had spoken to Shakespeare by phone from Australia, trying to explain to him what had happened, was happening. I belong in no tense, said Harold, and Shakespeare had replied, How can you. Harold was famous by association, though no one knew him, or recognised him. That was the only good bit of any of it. Of it. It.

He wanted back to relook. To redescribe it all. To himself? Self? An adoration of absurdity.

*

Grit and salt, dog shit and steam rising from early morning boilers. Skerricks of snow in terrace front gardens, shoeboxes of hope. He shuffles along, driving himself to cover vast distances. No sun has shown for days. Blackbirds are in mulchy leaflitter—last year's leaves, and beneath, the year's before, and beneath that murky territory between organic and inorganic . . . it's there the grubs are found, less than fat after winter, but there. And another of the disillusioned shuffles past, crazily clad but warmer than Harold, and saying, It's cost seven fuckin' quid what's a man supposed to do, I mean seven fuckin' quid what's a man supposed to do I MEAN SEVEN fuckin' quid . . . ! The scaffolding of trees threatening to bud but not quite there, though clumps of mistletoe look smugly down on him—no, I won't do that to them, he reassures himself, it's me that's smug. He detests his contrition, his rhizomic spreading into goodwill. He crosses the bridge and looks across at St John's and is perplexed by the intensity of the hairdo of the weeping willow. It lulls him, of course, of course. Not a punt on the river at this hour, just a single white swan centring the middle arch of a bridge, any bridge. The water looks unhealthy. He is not projecting. The sun would be well and truly up if it could break through, though still low to the horizon. He is watching blackbirds flit through a hedge—but they don't flit, head down, all intensity, they move decisively. The language is so pathetically inadequate he thinks, moving his mouth to make other sounds. His phone rings. He has a phone—his one concession to Lucida who he says was better when she was indifferent. He takes it out: a text: You okay? He fumbles, doesn't flit, across the keypad. Yeah. Then he adds, slowly, This is more environmentally destructive than any other human achievement. It gets everywhere insidiously. A conflict diamond in every hand. Then another. He types embarrassingly fast. Adding, This is no earth song. H.

He's on a street he knows well. Every day of every year he has known Cambridge, a dwelling is and has been renovated. There might be a hundred terraces and semi-detacheds on each side of the street. At any given time one, maybe two, is being renovated. It's a street in constant need. Of. Little dog on a leash pauses, shits in front of him. It's a well-cared for dog. Its possessor is well clad. She watches it shit and ignores Harold. The shit is left on the path to steam and declare.

He has wandered for half a day and not eaten. He pissed in a bush as cars went by. He was as discrete as he could manage. No one saw anything, he was sure. And now he's at Eddington, the new estate the university is conjuring out of farmland. He shuffles through the build—outside the new Sainsbury's superstore a line of hi-viz jacketed male workers, all with helmets on and smoking. The superstore is open but the only customers are workers. It is eerie walking through the squares and between the new buildings, some with bikes outside and workers sitting at desks, but mainly empty. He shuffles past another onlooker who says to Harold, The lemmings are moving here to bide their time. Harold says, Coming home to roost, more likely. He surprises himself at his outwardness, and shuffles off fast before the stranger can say anything to his *stranger*. And now he is back in front of the Sainsbury's. He goes in and buys a water and a banana. He is the only one at the till other than the employee. He looks back into the cavern of goods and says, So this is the new heart and soul. And she replies, it will be . . . we are the marketplace to the new. He tries to smile, as he respects her, but he can't. He finds an empty seat away from workers on smoko, and consumes the perishables of the world, wondering where to put the empty plastic bottle when finished, scanning the wreckage of the world beyond the neat and precise builds.

You walk on water you walk on brown water on flagstones the sludge between the cobbles this is walking in the rain and the east is drier the fens drier believe it or not; believe it or not the dunnocks in the hedgerows roused with the season the interjections of blackbirds and squirrels—grey squirrels with a dash of the old red—making the loping dash between bare trees though finding a heart of lime or oak or beech. Storage. This Brit nationalist squirrel-cull mentality he mutters to himself, shuffling over the spread over the flow, the seepage. Mallards on the ponds the white swans sailing outside the area drainable the regular flow of Granta and Cam, not the crucible of college waters. How can I belong? he says to a stranger, who gathers his collar and almost slips away. A picket line. Another picket line years later, and still the pension-stress the miserly retraction of old age into subservient compliance. Here am I, he says, standing with the picketers, who look oddly at him but he's another body another barrier standing with them. People cross the picket line with sideglances or snarls, some barrel through on bikes. Some say, I am just going to . . . Sorry, I am in a hurry. Stock epithets of indifference.

Crossing a road no cars slow down. It's too far to the next crossing which is just an opening then an island on a roundabout, nothing more. Take one's life. And the drip from overhanging evergreens almost religious in their ritual, the chandeliers in the conservative college on the river thrusting forth poetry like tolerance and innovation. The tricks of the trade.

He sees a machine, a screw as high as a tower, an augury into the earth, a building site foundations deep, a spiralling an unearthing. It is guttural and remorseless and florescent men stand around watching, adjusting their white helmets in timing with the calling up of sand and rock particles. Those new spaces they have created to reinvest with presence. All the layering identity calls on—the Neolithic, the iron age, the Roman, undertones they do and don't want. Why had he shuffled into Brixton Academy so long ago now to see even more than hear Forever England bellowed out before the Sex Pistols joined their own staging. Rotten snarling, 'There will be as long as we're around'. These Englander bigots—one of the undercurrents of punk. Harold had gone looking for Crass to find a way around, away, but their commune was not for the likes of.

Down the laneway past the pepperpot Newton buildings, he shuffles towards an oncoming bicycle, one just lifted from the road. A collision is inevitable. Snails are on the path and stretched earthworms losing form to transparency, stranded. He tries to help. The bike crashes into him. Watch out, OLD MAN—this place is inhabited by more than you. The tower of the UL is steaming—ominous with its subtexts which scholars are committedly disinterested in. Such is the dedication to knowledge-acquisition, selective dissemination. What of protest, what of Plautus, what of Erasmus, what of brilliant young people brandishing signs that can cast in so many directions. The signs. I am here, he says, to be under the signs. What can I do in their shadows, their long pall: '*Lupus est homo homini, non homo, quom qualis sit non novit . . .*'

It had been many years since Harold had been in a cab. Once, he'd been known by local taxi drivers as an interesting fare. But that was so many years ago. He is injured; somebody offers to phone Panther Cabs. To take him . . . where, nowhere. To take him to Shakespeare's? His only remaining friend. He could sleep with pennywhistles and dogs with dermatitis, he could share a coffee, but no alcohol now. All these mental illnesses ascribed, and he'd fit. A car with a cab driver who laments Brexit and Harold feels hope. From Pakistan twenty years ago—and now the imperialists want to undo the 'feedback' of their imperialism. Consequences, he spits that word and Harold spits with him. Whereto—to Shakespeare's . . . I, Timon, need a cave to call my own for a few days, my clavicle damaged. You sound very self-centred, says the driver, who also adds, No need to pay, old man. He then says: My home village was shelled recently in an exchange between armies, those manifestations of hate.

But Harold stops short of Shakespeare's and after the

cab has gone, struggles to a wall where he sits and waits for nothing. Not even chance. He looks over the road at some green space, the plastic hexagons through which grass grows—cells of mud and sketchy grass. Greener than the grass. Plastics. The surface has been remade to launch us to Mars, he thinks. People steer around him. His clavicle bothers him but he decides never to think about it again, no matter what.

A young person in a big jacket is speaking. They are non-binary, which makes Harold comfortable. He does not want binaries. He thinks of Lucida and says hello to them. Are you okay? I have dirty hands, he says, looking down at the dirt and abrasions. Would you like some gel to disinfect them, asks the young person. Being young seems relevant. It is vegan gel, says the stranger. I am not sure, says Harold, as a blob of thick liquid plonks into his palm and starts to sting his abrasions. Rub them together, says the person, And the gel will evaporate. Harold rubs his hands together and starring at them says, Hey presto! And then the young person exclaims, Hey, aren't you the poet . . . ? A wood-pigeon, ready to take off, is watching them cautiously from . . . what is it . . . A larch? Harold hears his thoughts spoken aloud by the other.

*

I met him—the poet—on the street in Cambridge last year. Maybe three months before he passed away. We spent a lot of time together. He was sitting on a wall studying . . . well, it was hard to tell what. He was bleeding. He'd been hit by a bike. He was half waiting for a friend, but it turned out the friend was sick himself and in Addenbrookes. I took him to visit his friend, Shakespeare. And then I discovered that his friend was in fact one of my ex-teachers. Shakespeare and tragedy paper. They kind of grunted at each other and didn't really form words, though the odd quote from *Timon of Athens* was swapped—I recognised that out of their weird code. Both were bitter men. I'd never seen my old teacher laugh, not once, not even when he was talking about Falstaff, and the poet—Harold—only grimaced. He told me the time he found most interesting and disturbing was evening, when light was in retreat. Most interesting as the sun set on low hills where he came from, the wheat bloody, and here when it set over fields and fens, entangling in the thin rows of trees and patches of woods around these fields, where pheasants erupted before settling; but disturbing with the winter rush homeward through cramped medieval streets with people colliding or almost colliding, and tourists desperate to be somewhere that mattered after ticking off the sights.

He asked me why my head was shaved at least a dozen times. He asked if I was unwell, he apologised. He knew why. I guess he was trying to make conversation. He said, I like it as a statement, though in Australia you'd have to worry about skin cancers. And I said, I would wear a hat if in Australia. And he said, Sorry, I am just being a dickhead. I never asked him about Lucida, though of course I knew. I did ask if he still wrote poetry, and he said, I will write one more poem. About what? I asked. Will you take me to the orchid house in your college? he asked. He loathed the university and colleges and yet he'd once been part of them.

He'd always wanted to see my college's orchid house. I took him. He wrote this poem, likely his last though I wasn't his keeper and who knows what might turn up.

Orchid House

He and I connect in passing maybe once or twice a year.
We walk through his garden realm and he tells me what's new,
what he and the other gardeners have been working with, coaxing.

Today, he took me into the orchid house which over all the many
years I've never visited, had no concrete vision of. And into the
    hot zone
we went, humidity and twenty-five degrees centigrade playing

with the vestiges of snow fibrillating *outside*. Orchids in their
    glorious
but uncomfortable being, stunning but disturbing flowering,
    withholding
time. *This one* in the hanging garden flowers below the plimsoll
    line,

a world on its head equilibrium in this contradictory system. It's
not hard to see why the obsession—the steady as it goes, the
    denying
of all that goes on outside, the waiting. Temperature, water,
    atmosphere

controlled. And the sweet odour—the lure and the fall, cataclysm
of enticement, those precise flowers wanting you or something of
    use.
But the one that grabbed my attention was a small specimen
    with emphatic

> bloom in a small pot—'Glacier Peak' with its brash white trumpet, its throaty declaring of vortex and immanence. John—nurturer, sensor of plants—knows its manifest ironies. And I, just appearing as if from nowhere, tune in fast searching for its frequency.
>
> Almost too eager?

I have no idea who the 'he' is. I asked him and he said, There's nothing to say . . . nothing to add. Though he did add, later, There are too many masters in Cambridge, and you don't need them . . . all this hullabaloo around the high priests of secular divination, all this claptrap around prophetic teachers. As long as there are students, this sort of thing will go on. He said that, and I agreed, some of my peers embarrassing me with their falling down to old patriarchies and thinking that they were risking all. We don't need it, but we perform, trapped in these ancient buildings of our desiring—our radicalism displaying manners in our most angry moments. From a position of privilege, we will rebel all to the better. What we say among ourselves is the ritual of denial. He said, Watch the ducks *inside* . . . they culled the Canada geese . . . lacking local colour, authenticity. Out of the blue, as we were sitting near the weir, he said, I was a gardener at one of the colleges for a while . . . well, not a gardener, but an assistant gardener . . . I raked and hoed and used the leaf blower, which I hated, and was the reason I quit. It was only a few weeks really, and I am not sure how many years ago it was now.

Sharp noises bothered him. Out of tune instruments bothered him, but he said that they made the best music. *In tune* is not creative.

He slept on my floor with a single blanket. He ate little—fruit, mainly. He was flatulent. He told me he was sexless when I asked him why he had no interest in me—he never made the slightest pass. He also said, It'd be borderline inappropriate even if I did desire you. I desire nothing. He said, I'd rather see—and feel—the redistribution of wealth in the world. We should own nothing. Then he added, I detest the word 'should'. He picked at scabs on his hands. He said, I love you for bothering—not with me per se, but just bothering. Love is better than desire. But they are fused, I said. You only think that because you are young, he said. Not that young, I said, I am twenty-six and two years into my PhD. He never asked me what my PhD was on, but he did ask if I wrote poetry. I try to, I said. He never asked to see or hear any. But he did read an essay I wrote on reclaiming fenland—on creating nature reserves from farmland. He said, This sings to me. He once accidentally brushed my bare arm and withdrew rapidly. Later, he said, You have beautiful skin and looked ashamed. I joked, It's post-colonial skin! but it made him look sad, defeated. I told him a ghost story from my village. He responded, They are real you know. I replied, I have no doubt at all. And then he was studying capsules of rain on the window. Your friends think you are odd having me here. I feel like a dirty old man. Fuck them, I said. And he said, I understand your need to say that. Lucida was once, briefly, like that . . . in the flush of it all, her father a distant thought.

My story? I was born on an island. An English father—white—and an islander mother—not white. People made a trajectory for me and I resisted. And yet I am here, at the centre of privilege as the echoes of Brexit make fuel for anger in many white working-class houses. Ukip is at my heals, and yet, I am British. They hate that more than anything, and Harold loved it more than anything. Love me? Yes, maybe a little.

I ride a bike—all over. But one afternoon it was stolen from outside the Faculty of Classics cast gallery. I had been studying a broken penis on a broken statue. And then I went out to get my bike, pick up some food, and return to Harold, who would be stretched out on the floor doing nothing, just staring at the ceiling or window. It was gone. I walked home and burst into tears. He dragged himself up, and said I will sort something. I insisted I go with him, but he said NO, and shuffled out. That evening he was back and called me out in the muffled growl of his, and there was my bike. Not any bike, not a bike like my bike, but my actual bike. The chain had been cut with bolter cutters, but he had that too. Maybe you can get it fixed? he said. He wouldn't be drawn further, and went back to lying prostrate on the floor, under that thin blanket.

One morning, I stood there naked so he could see me. He said, You are undergoing a change? Hormones? Surgery? I asked what he meant, adding, That would suggest that I was choosing a gender, but I am not. But I would be proud to do so if I wished or felt the need. You do not understand . . . we are always changing. He looked at me and said, You are very beautiful. Thanks, I said, with a certain gratitude which I offended myself with . . . No, this is the way I was made and this is the way I will stay . . . I mean, If I wanted to go one way or another I would, but

I don't want to. I belong to me and the earth. You are an earth song, he said.

*

Those notes over the score—there is a way to play it, and I am telling you. Emphasise the percussion here and here! What is that damned noise? The foundations being driven deep. I cannot stand hammer blow on hammer blow, those parodies of permanence. In my temporariness I am subjected to repetitive sounds of the machine age that go right through my body. I am being wiped out by industrialism, by the economics of dwelling.

*

Sunshine breaks through. Daffodils in the college garden beds. Moss on stone stretching, becoming aware that soon, in months to come, it might fall. All is alive, he said. Holding their arm, he struggled past Sainsbury's. A young woman with a dog rugged up, in a sleeping bag, guitar next to her, was reading *The Brothers Kamazarov*. He spoke to her. He gave her ten pounds. I didn't think you had any money, they said. I don't, he said. A little further down near the entry to Waterstones, a young man playing guitar—sides of head shaved, in an army surplus jacket, reading a broken-spined novel spread before him while strumming. What are you reading? asks Harold, who has no more money to give. I am reading *The Idiot*, he said. You're are a beautiful person, said Harold. I feel I should ask you for a blessing, said the young man, laughing. There was no sarcasm, so Harold responded, You already have it, mate. We're all part of the rapture. Even Boris Johnson? asked the young man. Harold laughed and his ribs hurt, he gripped their arm harder.

*

Before I came here—before the first time—I crossed back & forth across the Nullarbor. I stayed out at Cook, feeling I was intruding on no one's stolen land. I felt it was the only place I could be. But that was a simplistic hope, a hope to sidestep colonialism, and I couldn't. I watched wedge-tailed eagles make towers in nests, I drank in the bluebush from mirages, I scratched the soles of my feet on limestone karst. The residues of the atomic tests everywhere, no matter what the claims of wind directions. The dingoes edged and I loved the howling. It was then I remembered hearing Mahler as a small child with my mother, my father gone. I remember it all but bits had been erased. I lifted the rewrites, the scratchings out, and accessed the fair copies. It was all there, and I heard it on the Nullarbor, and I knew that was wrong, the caverns beneath my feet aching with my alien gall. Have you seen the fens burning with a fire that can't be extinguished? There's that, too. The overlays we feed on, that comparisons we make our literary lies from. Poetry was a trigger moment over and over for me, especially when I hide from the page. I fed the schism of text. I crossed out and made louder in my own image.

A lone snowy owl is being watched in Norfolk, fixated on by well-wishers.

*

When I slept on the streets in London, down near the river, opposite what is now the London Eye, I spent the days in my sleeping bag, cocooned in trauma, wondering if anyone would kick me, locked off in my world of sherry, the off-licence my point of reference, trying to make poems where no poems would come. I would doze off dreaming of Lucida and worried about what fame and power were doing to her. I saw echidnas in the weird blue-green light of suffocation I opened my eyes to, the traffic and oil fumes a synaesthesia I set my metonymies of dislocation by. At night, sometimes, leaving my patch vulnerable to occupation, I walked . . . as far as Hackney where I found conversation and food. He said, she said, he said, she said. I understood the away and the where we are now. I respected.

There's a lie in the British Library you must have seen. The 'paranoid reading of Shakespeare's poem . . .' by the 'crazy' letter writer. The ironies of the colonial don't shake any British establishment foundations. The implicated self and Queen. Here, Edward laid a stone cyclopean in size. Haven't you wondered why the imperialists look to Homer for the answers in peace and war and war and war. Their peace is a desire in the maintaining of the spoils.

Lucida once said to me, All these Rosencrantzes and Guildensterns we believe serve the powers that crush us are themselves being crushed. These courtiers without rights who will do all the dirty work because they have no choice. My sleeping bag was no cocoon, but it did incubate the pain of all who passed saying things in its earshot they normally wouldn't say. The servants of industry and the state deplore their own condition.

*

I couldn't make sense of his 'ravings' over those last days. His desire for a forest burial, to have an oak planted over him that would send down rhizomes and convert him to plant matter. Not the plant feeding on the animal, but the plant just working its way round to the mineral. He said I will be the poem, the only worthwhile enscripting. He called for people: the Sab Woman… the Woman and Child… and with a frightening virulence, The Stalker. He often mentioned Shakespeare. And Mahler.

*

There was a pair of geese. There were geese, two. Working their way along the concrete walkway on the south side of the Thames. People were swinging in the power station—literally swinging. An art statement. An art statement directed by men, constraining women; constrained by 'art', that refuge of tyranny. The geese were trying to avoid the bikes which made seeing London easier, more spontaneous. Someone played a guitar, but it was a past tense. *And he said,* Lucida was an artist, not an actor, wasn't she? But she did both in those different lives, fuelled by a diminishing mountain of iron ore, cleared vegetation. But she also claimed to be *also* from a relatively 'poorer' background, listening to harsh music, a fan, follower who wanted the key to the labyrinth. Wasn't she? That's what her promo claims. All of these. Ten francs a day was better than five. You know. The excess of seeing. How much sense it makes in the parsing. How a guest manages in the circumstances. They were male and female, really. And the narrative threads through the feathering—what each lost quill tells. But who cares from where they fall, which part of flight or covering, which signature of life cycle of the star-struck, the cosmology of the apex of roof of the Hackney Empire, so far away across the roofs, the curved and straight streets, the empty occupy space outside St Paul's where Scotland the Brave is piped to the constabulary celebrating Pentonville Prison as an act, the clergyman in his kit saying, I will find out, but I won't be coming back out to tell you. These scriptures of Milton and an unwavering commitment to a republican declaration. Yes, a pair of geese.

He said, to a stranger: I agree up to a point, but I disagree re the lack of philosophical depth (as implied) . . . I think Hamlet rejigged 'contemplation' and introspection as disruption (and rupture in the textuality)—really, the whitepress shows a non-understanding of that tension (and the nature of the fatalistic 'comic'—its dissolving . . . its bleakness). Further, further . . . the body count in the shadow of the absurdity of powerlust sadly makes complete sense. And now the witless jester—one of the troupe of—from Australia wants to give sanctuary to Apartheid residues of farmacology . . . the white farmering of Aboriginal land with the experienced Cape warriors of purity . . . the growers . . .' And he cried, and his shoulder ached, and he leant . . . on me.

*

It was then, only then, then, only, only then that he realised or accepted he was a construction of Lucida with only a smidgen of agency. Nothing to do with her granting him this, just what was, what he'd managed to extract from his privilege his assumptions his feet on the ground, the dirt anathema for all his love of 'nature'. She had been there and seen the uses he put her to, shapeshifting and roleplaying to suit his gameplan, his 'letting her be' who she wanted, as some kind of Derridean gift. That *womaniser*, let it be said. Though so much more to him than that, out of Algeria, the persecution. Lucida admired his desire for signs, his reaching into Judaism for answers, and his love of the Palestinian people. But mostly his rejection of all states, of all governments, which she had manipulated for the sake of fate and destiny, to give purpose to an atheism. A cosmology of art for art's sake. She allowed him to deplore this, to love the feather as the feather. He accepted Lucida didn't need to love her own creations, subsets of everything as they were, are. *Benedictus benedicat.*

*

Memory loss is such an immaculate occurrence. A spring can't come again in predictable ways, and seasons don't fit the song rituals. Smell the coal and the grit and the salt dust and the cold, then the soft rain that drags you into the swirl, the spiralling. A drain that takes, and clogs. The swan on its volcanic nest, neck tucked. How do you recall your commune days, the cockatoos in flooded gums, the winter creek, the excrement that settles under firebreaks? These territories of habitats not yours, these declarations of survey you don't want to remember. All this out of the blue-grey, the novel I write out of your gendered life. I disown my heritage of genes, no chromosomes fit the staircase to the empty eye sockets of stolen women, the art franchise of modernity. Now, I-we-you are unmodern. The physicists were the first to walk into people, before mobile phones took away the seeing ahead unmediated, direct vision.

Why would you expect 'language to break down' as death approaches? I mean, it was always me, wasn't it, and my algorithms go outside the person you can ID, the profile in amongst the metadata. What do we do with this, breath steaming in an increasingly cold room—I have no visible means of support, a contested space. Where is the question in this, any of this? I drink cloudy apple juice from a fridge, a cross a road where the traffic won't break, resist my passing through, over. He *says*, Their cars are their gods. Together, the industry, is the Godhead. Nothing astounding there, but to bother saying so when few other words can form carries some emphasis. He *said*, My poetry was always about the emphatic. Somebody is grinding coffee beans nearby, inside, out of sight, though maybe they are looking at a robin from a window.

*

He talked of red-capped robins as sparks 'where I come from, where I can't belong—on stolen land . . . I am not worthy to speak of any of it'. He wasn't being arch or rhetorical or glib or overinflated—he just lacked the words, as all poets do, really.

*

No friend-group. No. No singularity. No unified theory to give us, to make our escape by. Little or less he gives us.

*

He spoke not of a culture but respected the fact and choice and necessity of culture. He declared he had none, nor wanted one, though was the product of ungoing cultural pressures and expectations. He did not subscribe though respected belief. He removed his shoes. He would not eat what was expected to show deference or respect if it involved the consuming of animals. That was his line. He did not. I did not with him. I said this struggle to be me-us extends all the way to the breathing and the breathless.

*

Late sun under cloud captured in bare willow strands, tongue-lashing quietly. Dunnocks, robins, a magpie. Ducks on the grass. So many chasing the sun.

*

His manuscripts—how to read, how to perform, how to

dismiss overwritten in red and blue pencil. His poems of his long period of silence. He would laugh at that—the pretentious self-serving egoism of 'silence'. It wasn't silence, it was loud, reverberating tormenting self-admonishing. The bullshit. The poems he collectively called *The Mahler Erasures* which he said were nothing to do with Mahler but everything to do with listening, in the same way Mahler had made from listening. From hearing inside and out. He had scribbled poems even when he said he couldn't or wouldn't.

*

He said: If anything of mine surfaces, send it to Calais in material and spiritual fact, and in metaphor. The disgrace of the wealthy, of the accumulators, of the exclusionists. Send it to the men of Manus island detention camp, send it to all those stuck in the limbo created by greed. It's not a worthiness, but a necessity. The seeing of it as worthiness is being inside the problem, of dismissing through mockery. Seagulls are flying over the river, not following its line.

*

Repetition.
Refrain.
Motif.

That's all this is, nothing more. The story is a loop. Daffodils are still being managed to appear. The dabbling ducks are still trying to speak for themselves.

*

And so. And so. And so. The overfamiliar isn't a clear picture: the evergreens at the back to the side the riverside of the Round Church. The bunched-up cluster of tombstones. They buy me some Bute Island vegan cheese from the health shop, and some bread, and we lean against the damp wall and eat. Crowds flow, voices erupt, phones are checked. In one of the old colleges, which one can't be remembered, a horse prepares to trot across the lawn. Always preparing—to trot, to prance, to display. Or speak in a bronze language we won't understand. But mostly, it's heat in my head and eucalyptus fumes signing off. Beneath the stones, the concrete, the dirt. The poets I have most respected are aware of what's beneath. They write with their hands, literally their hands. And now I am chasing the diminishing dot in my head—a singularity, I hope. I hope. Thankyou. All.

John Kinsella is a prize-winning Australian writer, poet, and environmental activist. His work includes *Peripheral Light: Selected and New Poems*, *Jam Tree Gully*, and *Drowning in Wheat: Selected Poems* and *Insomnia*. He has written numerous works of fiction and criticism, and taught poetry and literature all over the world. He is a Fellow of Churchill College, Cambridge University, and Emeritus Professor of Literature and Environment at Curtin University, Perth. Kinsella has received many awards for his poetry, including the Western Australian Premier's Book Award, the John Bray Award for Poetry, and the Australian Prime Minister's Literary Award for Poetry. He has won fellowships from the Literature Board of the Australia Council. Founding editor of the journal Salt in Australia, he served as international editor at the *Kenyon Review*.

Printed in the USA
CPSIA information can be obtained
at www.ICGtesting.com
JSHW020232010724
65634JS00003B/3